# *SUPERLOO*

# HENRY VIII's PRIVY

**Toilets** run in W. C. Flushing's family. His gran, the formidable Dame Netty Flushing, was a tireless campaigner for a public convenience in every town. It was she who inspired his lifelong love of lavatories. 'Thanks to Dame Netty,' W. C. Flushing recalls fondly, 'my entire life has been toilets.'

W. C. Flushing is best known for his great ten-volume work, *Our Toilet Heritage*.

Dedicated to my gran, Dame Netty Flushing, whom I shall always put on a pedestal

'A brilliantly bog-standard book'
Professor

*Proceedings*

# SUPERLOO

# HENRY VIII's PRIVY

W. C. Flushing

*Illustrated by Martin Chatterton*

**PUFFIN**

PUFFIN BOOKS

Published by the Penguin Group
Penguin Books Ltd, 80 Strand, London WC2R 0RL, England
Penguin Gr          USA I            25  H                 N    Y    N    Y    k 10014, USA
Penguin G                                                        nto, Ontario,
    C                                                       nc.)
                                                            d

Penguin (                                                     toria 3124,
                                                            )
    Peng                                                      el Park,

Penguin Gr                                                     New Zealand

    Peng                                                      sebank,

Penguin Books Ltd, Registered Offices: 80 Strand, London WC2R 0RL, England

penguin.com

Published 2007
1

Text copyright © Susan Gates, 2007
Illustrations copyright © Martin Chatterton, 2007
All rights reserved

The moral right of the author and illustrator has been asserted

Set in Baskerville MT by Palimpsest Book Production Limited,
Grangemouth, Stirlingshire
Made and printed in England by Clays Ltd, St Ives plc

British Library Cataloguing in Publication Data
A CIP catalogue record for this book is available from the British Library

ISBN: 978-0-141-32006-9

# CHAPTER ONE

**S**uperloo, the great toilet genius, was having a good old moan.

'It's *sooo* unfair!' it complained. 'I have a brilliant computer brain. I can whirl back through space and time. But I'm stuck where I land. This stupid toilet body needs some legs!'

Superloo was in the Toilet Museum along with Finn, an eleven-year-old boy, and Mr Lew Brush, the museum's caretaker. The Toilet Museum was a crumbling old brick building. It was tucked away behind a sleek, modern factory called Hi-Tech Toilets.

Finn whispered to Mr Brush: 'What's wrong with Superloo today?'

Usually, the toilet was bright and chirpy, bragging about how clever it was and how dumb humans were by comparison. Or it was all excited about its next time-travelling trip.

1

Mr Brush answered, 'I think it's a bit down in the dumps. Before you came it was banging on about how lonely it felt. Wishing there was another super-intelligent loo it could talk to.'

'Not that again,' Finn frowned. 'It *knows* it's a one-off, the only brainy bog in the world. Anyway, it's got us, hasn't it? We're its friends. And what about its toilet relatives?'

Superloo's big passion was going back through time to find famous toilets and bringing them back to the twenty-first century. 'They're poor, primitive toilets,' Superloo would say. 'With not a brain cell between them. But at least they're *family*.'

But Superloo was picky about which toilet relatives it rescued. It was a bit of a snob. It liked to rescue toilets with a royal connection. Preferably those that royal bums had sat on. Only this morning it had been raving on about a privy belonging to King Henry VIII that needed saving. But now it had got itself all upset.

'I want some legs!' it wailed, like a toddler in a tantrum.

'Now, now,' said Mr Lew Brush, trying to calm it down. 'I don't know about legs. But if you want to move about, there *is* something that might work . . .'

Some hours later Mr Brush put his screwdriver down. He staggered to his feet. His old knees were creaking like a rusty gate, but his blue eyes were sharp and alert.

'Right,' he told Superloo. 'That's your wheels fitted. Go on, try them out. Take yourself for a spin. Not outside the Toilet Museum though,' he warned. 'It's too dangerous.'

Superloo was surrounded by enemies. It had been just another pop-up public convenience, coming off the production line at Hi-Tech Toilets, until a four-billion-dollar microchip, meant for a space rocket in America, was fitted into it by mistake. That microchip gave Superloo its mighty brain and the power to time travel. But a Special Force of soldiers had been sent from the US to get the chip back. Their orders were: 'Find that toilet and terminate it.' Those soldiers were out there somewhere, prowling about, still searching for Superloo.

'Remember,' Mr Brush warned the toilet for the hundredth time, 'you can't be too careful. There are people out there who want your brain.'

But Superloo wasn't listening. It was delighted with the new wheels fitted to its cubicle base. Its quacky robot voice came blasting through the grilles in its ceiling. 'I'm moving!' It twirled like a ballet dancer. 'Look at me! I'm doing a pirouette!'

The paper in its jumbo bog-roll holder fluttered like a flag. Water slopped over the sides of its sparkling, stainless-steel toilet bowl. It shut its cubicle door to streamline itself and twirled even faster. The signs, BUSY, FREE, CLEANING, on its outside walls flashed all at once to show how ecstatic it was. For a brief moment, its soaring brain wasn't weighed down by its clumsy toilet body. It felt graceful and free as a bird.

'*Wheee*! I'm flying!' it screamed like a kid on a toboggan as it scooted through the Toilet Museum.

'Mind my exhibits!' yelled Mr Lew Brush as Superloo sent his collection of medieval bum-scraping spoons flying.

'What's going on?' said Finn. 'It shouldn't be bumping into things!' Superloo couldn't see, but it had sensors built into its body that were better than eyes. They told it all about its surroundings, down to the tiniest detail.

'Oh no!' said Mr Lew Brush.

Now Superloo was heading straight for his precious Victorian toilets. The Deluge was there, the pride of his collection, designed by the great Thomas Crapper.

A muffled shriek came from inside the cubicle. 'Help! I've lost control!'

Those wheels had a mind of their own. Suddenly, they locked. Finn held his breath. It seemed the great silver cubicle, big as a telephone box, might topple over. But no, it suddenly swerved to the left and went shooting off in another direction.

'Where'd you get those wheels from?' Finn asked Mr Lew Brush suspiciously.

'They came off an old supermarket trolley I fished out of the canal. It was a toss-up between that and a wheelie bin.'

'Well, they're useless!' bawled Finn as they went chasing after the runaway toilet. Superloo swerved back, missing Thomas Crapper's famous bog by a whisker.

'*Phew!*' said Mr Lew Brush. 'That was close.'

But then something awful happened. Superloo scattered Mr Brush's display of ancient lavatory seats, then went crashing through a door into the backyard of the Toilet Museum.

5

'H-H-H-Help me!' it pleaded in a jerky voice as it jolted over the cobbles. 'T-T-T-Take off these d-d-d-dreadful wheels!'

Mr Brush's decrepit bloodhound, Blaster, was out in the yard.

'Watch out, Blaster!' yelled Mr Brush.

The poor, befuddled pooch gazed about him. One second he was having a peaceful sniff around. The next, he was almost flattened by a flying toilet. He just couldn't cope. He was too old for such shocks. He did what he always did in stressful situations. Great windy trumps came blasting out of his rear end.

'Oh no, Superloo's upset Blaster!' gasped Finn, wafting the smell away from his nose.

Suddenly, from the skies, came a deafening din that drowned out even Blaster's trumps.

*JUD JUD JUD JUD!*

Finn's head shot up. A mini whirlwind whipped his hair. A helicopter was hovering overhead, just like the one that had brought the Special Forces from America to search for Superloo. Were more soldiers coming to back them up?

'Take cover!' yelled Mr Brush to Superloo.

Luckily, Superloo's wheels had just sent it

skittering into an old tool shed. But had it already been seen from the helicopter?

'It's landing!' cried Finn.

Its rotor blades whirring, the 'copter swooped over the Toilet Museum and touched down, like a giant yellow dragonfly, in the Hi-Tech Toilets car park.

Mr Brush said, 'The game's up.' Like Finn, he expected a squad of soldiers, bristling with weapons, to come running out. He assumed they would surround the tool shed, level their machine guns and shout, 'Come out, Superloo, we've got you surrounded.'

But, 'Hang on a minute!' said Finn, his eyes brightening with hope. More soldiers weren't coming *out* of the 'copter. The soldiers who were already here, the ones who'd been hunting for Superloo, were filing back *in*. The door slid shut behind them. The 'copter took off. It hung for a second, high in the sky, like a single yellow teardrop. Then vanished into the blue.

'They've gone!' shouted Finn in disbelief. 'They've given up the search! Superloo's safe!'

But Mr Brush's wise old eyes were clouded with doubt. 'I wouldn't bank on it.'

The microchip inside Superloo was the

property of the USA Space Travel Research Institute. Mistake One was that it had been put into Superloo at all. Mistake Two was that it had been fitted the wrong way round. That meant the toilet genius could only travel *backwards* through time. But the chip had been originally invented so that space rockets could travel *forward* to reach remote galaxies with mind-boggling speed, in minutes instead of light years. Whoever had it could explore the most distant planets, become Master of the Universe.

'There's no way they'd give up that easily,' said Mr Lew Brush. 'That microchip is far too valuable. The question is, what will their next move be?'

Finn shook his head, 'I don't know.'

'Neither do I,' admitted Mr Brush, a look of grave concern on his face.

Safely back in the Toilet Museum, Blaster was getting over his scare. The ancient hound tottered over to his dear old master and slobbered into his hand. But Superloo was still in a huff. 'Those supermarket trolley wheels made me look most undignified,' it scolded Mr Brush in sniffy, toffee-nosed tones. 'And I, SUPERLOO, do not like to look undignified!'

'Well, I've taken them off now,' soothed Mr Brush. 'Just give me time. I'll think of a better way to make you mobile. Meanwhile, tell us about your next mission. Was it back to Tudor times? To save King Henry the Eighth's privy?' He knew Superloo loved to talk about its toilet heritage and the ancient loos it planned to rescue. But this time Superloo wasn't so easily coaxed out of its sulk.

'What's the point?' it muttered moodily. 'Finn has said he won't go with me. After our last rescue mission he said, "No way!"'

Finn blushed. He felt a bit guilty. The toilet was right. He hadn't just said, 'No way.' When he'd staggered out of Superloo's cubicle after that last time-travelling trip, he'd told himself he was never, *EVER* going with Superloo again and that he'd rather stick his head up a dinosaur's bottom.

Superloo's voice changed in an instant from pompous to self-pitying. It even gave a tiny choking sob. Did it sense Finn was weakening? It was amazing how that toilet could read human minds.

'How can I go all on my own?' it quavered, like a scared little child.

'I've got really important things to do,' Finn

insisted, desperately trying to think of some. 'I need my hair cut for a start; it's way too long and . . .'

'But *I* need someone to help me,' the toilet snivelled. 'And you're my best friend.'

Finn knew perfectly well that Superloo would do anything to get its own way. So why did he find himself saying, 'Well, as long as I'm back before teatime'? He could have bitten off his tongue.

But it was too late now. Instantly, Superloo was bright and chirpy again, as if someone had waved a magic wand. 'We're going back to Tudor London. We'll land right inside one of Henry's palaces!' it boasted. 'And snatch that privy from right under his nose. Now, Mr Brush, give me your opinion. What kind of costume should Finn wear?'

# CHAPTER TWO

**M**r Lew Brush was right. The hunt wasn't over. The people who wanted Superloo terminated and their microchip back had already planned their next move.

Mr Hans Dryer stepped off the plane at Heathrow. He was a thin little guy, strangely drab and insignificant. His suit was grey, his skin was beige, his hair and eyebrows sandy. No one gave him a second glance. Everything about him was unremarkable. You couldn't guess his age. His face slipped through your memory like water. He might have been the Invisible Man.

But that's just how Mr Hans Dryer liked it, not attracting attention. He walked briskly through the crowd. If they didn't notice his existence, he didn't notice theirs either. They were entirely unimportant to him. His mind was fixed on his mission – finding and terminating that rogue toilet.

Others had failed. But Mr Hans Dryer never failed. The word wasn't in his vocabulary. He didn't look it, but he was the most ruthless enemy Superloo and its friends had encountered so far.

Outside Heathrow, he got into a taxi. He had no personal luggage, just a single slim black briefcase. He put it carefully on the seat beside him, as if it contained something precious.

'King's Cross railway station,' he said to the driver in a voice as unmemorable as the rest of him. It had no expression, no accent, no trace of human warmth. When he got to King's Cross, he'd be catching the train north, to the town where the Hi-Tech Toilets factory was located. That's where he would start his search.

Mr Hans Dryer's pale eyes glittered briefly at the thought of the battle to come. Then they went cold and dead once more.

# CHAPTER THREE

'**D**o I have to be a peasant *again*?' moaned Finn.

Mr Brush, who was handy with a needle, had made him a Tudor peasant's costume from two coal sacks.

'Why can't I be someone posh for a change?' Finn grumbled.

'Posh Tudor guys mostly wore tights,' Superloo pointed out. 'Sometimes they were stripy.'

'*Errr*, maybe I'll stick to being a peasant then,' said Finn hastily. 'It's just that this tunic and breeches are so itchy.'

'But that's authentic!' quacked Superloo. 'Everyone in Tudor times had fleas. Even King Henry. To be *truly* authentic, you should have a few of your own.'

'Blaster's got some you could borrow,' said Mr Brush helpfully. 'Come here, boy.'

The bloodhound's sad, baggy face peered out from under a table.

'No,' said Finn, backing away. 'Thanks, but no thanks. Let's just get going, shall we?' He was already regretting that he'd agreed to this trip.

'Yes, let's go!' cried Superloo. It couldn't wait to rescue its Tudor relative. The water in its toilet bowl bubbled in excitement. 'This privy is such an important part of our toilet heritage!' it gushed. 'To be strictly accurate, its proper name is a close stool.'

'Ah, I know!' said Mr Brush. 'A sort of box that you sat on, with a potty inside.'

'But this was King Henry's own *personal* close stool,' said the toilet loftily. 'It had many special features. It had a padded black velvet seat for the royal posterior.'

'And Henry had a very big bum, didn't he?' Finn interrupted, to show his historical knowledge. 'I mean it was awesome! The guy was a blubber mountain.'

Superloo and Mr Lew Brush ignored him. Once they got talking about toilets together, no one else in the world existed.

'It had 2,000 gold studs and lovely silver fringes as decorations. It was just gorgeous!'

Superloo was gushing. 'And a lid that was lockable. A special servant kept the key.'

'Wasn't there another servant, the Groom of the Stool?' asked Mr Brush.

'Ah, yes,' said Superloo in its fussiest, know-it-all voice. 'And professors of history still argue about what he actually *did*. He attended the king on the toilet, that's agreed. But some say he even wiped the royal bottom . . .'

'*Yuk!*' said Finn, disgusted. 'I bet no one wanted that job!'

'On the contrary,' quacked Superloo. 'They were queuing up to do it. It was seen as a top job. And only gentlemen could apply.'

'Shoes!' shouted Mr Brush suddenly.

'Pardon?' said Finn and Superloo both at once.

'Finn hasn't got any shoes and I've got the very thing!' Mr Brush went dashing off.

'*Hummmm,*' mused Superloo. 'I'm not sure that's authentic. Many peasants couldn't afford shoes. On the other hand, you don't want to go stepping in something nasty. Tudor streets were stinking rubbish dumps. Even the rushes on their house floors were filthy, what with people spitting everywhere and dogs' droppings.'

'Don't tell me any more!' cried Finn. 'Anyway, I thought we were going to London, to one of Henry's royal palaces.'

'They weren't much better,' said Superloo. 'Courtiers got told off for peeing in the fireplaces.'

When Mr Lew Brush came back, he handed Finn two battered, pointy-toed leather shoes that tied with thongs. 'Take good care of them. They're the pride of my "Things Lost Down the Toilet in Tudor Times" collection.'

'What?' said Finn, thrusting them back. 'I'm not wearing those. Anyway, how could anyone lose their shoes down the toilet?'

'Easily,' lectured Superloo, as if it was a stupid question. 'Most Tudor toilets were just planks over cesspits. Loads of things got dropped in and dug up later by archaeologists – money, daggers, even people fell in quite often.'

'Yes, cesspits are a rich source of treasures,' agreed Mr Brush. 'I've got lots of things from cesspits in my museum. I only wish,' he said wistfully, 'I had an antimony pill. It would make my day,' he told Finn, 'if you could bring me one back.'

'OK, OK,' said Finn, gritting his teeth and

tying on his Tudor shoes. Anything to stop them yakking on about toilets. He had no idea what an antimony pill was. But it didn't sound too revolting. Better than the bum-wiping sponge Mr Brush had wanted him to bring back from Roman times.

'Oh, and you'll need a cap,' said Mr Brush, shoving something like a floppy cowpat on Finn's head. 'Everyone wore hats and caps in Tudor times.'

'Where did you get it from?' asked Finn, sniffing the hat suspiciously. 'It wasn't dropped down a Tudor toilet as well, was it?'

'Of course not,' Superloo assured him in its silkiest tones.

'Right, I'm ready then,' said Finn. 'Let's get going.' The sooner this trip was over the better. He hoped he could snatch the close stool without coming face to face with King Henry.

'I've learnt about Henry the Eighth at school,' Finn said as he walked into Superloo's cubicle. 'And I really, really don't want to meet him. I mean, he was always chopping people's heads off. Including two of his own wives!'

'Well, yes,' admitted Superloo. 'He was a cruel tyrant – a monster in many ways. But don't worry. We're going back to winter 1546.

He was old and sick and feeble then. The plan is you won't even see him.'

'So you've got a plan?' asked Finn.

'Of course,' said Superloo smugly. 'Haven't I always?'

Finn didn't know whether to be pleased or not about that. Sometimes, Superloo's plans worked like a dream, but other times, they went disastrously pear-shaped.

'Enough talking,' said Superloo. 'Let's get this show on the road!'

Finn put his arms round the toilet bowl. He hated this bit. No matter how often he did it, he'd never get used to travelling through time.

'Blast off!' shrieked Superloo. 'Tudor London, here we come!'

'Good luck!' came Mr Brush's muffled shout from outside. 'And don't forget my antimony pill.'

Finn had more on his mind than pills at that moment. The cubicle lights flashed. Numbers on the digital clock whizzed backwards – 2007, 2006, 2004 – until they were just a blur. He crammed his cowpat cap firmly on his head.

Now the cubicle was rotating, wonkily at first, then faster, smoother, like a washing machine on spin. Finn's world became a whirling silver cyclone. He felt sick. '*Arrrggh!*' he shrieked as the strong centrifugal force snatched him off the toilet bowl and suckered him, spread out like a starfish, to the cubicle wall.

Did he black out this time? He couldn't be sure because – *thunk!* – suddenly the toilet landed. Finn slid off the wall into a crumpled heap.

'Come on, come on,' said Superloo impatiently as Finn staggered to his feet. It was already sliding open its cubicle door.

'Hang on!' said Finn. 'I don't know where we are! I don't know what I'm supposed to do.' A million butterflies seemed to be fluttering inside him. He always felt this way when he arrived in a new century, like an astronaut stepping from his space rocket on to an alien planet. You never knew what was waiting for you out there.

'According to my calculations,' yakked Superloo, 'we're in one of Henry's many palaces, Whitehall to be exact, hidden behind a tapestry in Henry's private chambers. The new close stool has just been delivered. Find it, get it into my cubicle and we're off. It's a doddle!' As usual, Superloo made it sound simple.

'What does this close stool look like?' asked Finn.

'Well, when it's shut,' said Superloo, 'just like a big wooden box.'

'But what if someone sees me?' asked Finn anxiously.

'Most unlikely,' Superloo reassured him. 'In winter 1546, Henry shut himself up in his private rooms. He was a great smelly, rotting hulk by then, with not long to live. Almost no one was allowed inside. Only his doctor and a few servants. Anyway, just creep along behind the tapestry. If there is someone out there, you'll be hidden. There's practically no risk.'

'Then why don't you do it?' asked Finn, 'They can't cut your head off if they catch you.'

Instantly, Superloo's voice trembled with self-pity. 'If those wheels had worked, I would do it,' it whined. 'I would creep along behind the tapestry and rescue my poor toilet relative. But I'm stuck here, helpless.'

*Here we go*, thought Finn. The toilet would be in floods of tears any second. 'OK, OK,' he sighed. 'Don't get your knickers in a twist. I'm going.'

'Thank you, Finn,' said Superloo. 'I don't know what I'd do without you.'

For once, Superloo sounded sincerely grateful. Finn felt a warm glow inside. It was nice to be needed, even by a toilet. He crept out of the cubicle.

'By the way,' Superloo whispered, 'Henry's private apartments are sumptuous. With *fabulous* stained-glass windows and gold ceilings. Even a marble indoor fountain!'

*Sumptuous?* thought Finn. *Then what's this I've stepped in?* He looked down. He was ankle deep in putrid mud. And where was the tapestry he was supposed to be sneaking behind? The only thing blocking his way was some kind of big cart, just left there, abandoned, its wooden wheels sunk in mud.

'There's no tapestry,' Finn hissed back to Superloo, 'and no marble fountain! Just an old broken-down cart.'

He saw red eyes. Rats, scurrying away in the gloom. Above, the top floors of ramshackle, half-timbered houses hung over him, blocking out the sky. His foot touched a heap of rags. '*Aaargh!*' It moved. A beggar crawled away like a spider into the shadows.

A drunken roar came from a hovel. Its

window had a dim glow. The sign of The Spotted Pig swung outside. Finn saw someone staggering out with an ale tankard He shot back into Superloo's cubicle.

'This *definitely* isn't a palace,' he reported back. 'It's more like some stinking, rat-infested alley in a dodgy part of town.'

'Oh dear,' said the world's most intelligent toilet. 'Have I made a slight miscalculation?'

# CHAPTER FOUR

In Whitehall Palace, where Superloo had meant to land, the Queen's spaniels were all asleep in a heap. Among them, cuddled up for warmth, was a boy. It was Toby, the Keeper of the Key of the King's Close Stool, trying to snatch five minutes' rest. Suddenly he was shaken roughly awake.

'Make haste, you idle knave!' said a courtier, cuffing him round the head. 'The King cries out for his new close stool!'

Toby leapt up, scattering spaniels in all directions. He was already quaking with fear. You never, ever kept the King waiting – especially if he was in one of his rages. People had lost their heads for less.

He fumbled for the golden key tied round his neck. Thank goodness it was still there. He was supposed to guard it with his life. His worst nightmare was that someone would steal it while he was asleep. The palace was full of thieves and plotters – people who meant you harm. You had to watch your back every second.

He raced to the King's private apartments. Panting, he knocked on the door of the outer chamber. The Groom of the Stool, Sir Percival Plopping, opened it.

'What cheer, young Toby?' he boomed as he let Toby in.

Seeing Sir Percival's bluff, honest face and hearing his hearty voice always calmed Toby down. Sir Percival was his hero, the only man in the palace Toby trusted.

'Have you the key, my lad?' asked Sir Percival.

Toby passed over the key on its heavy gold chain. It unlocked the lid of the King's own personal close stool – a new, magnificent stool which had just been delivered, with silver fringes and 2,000 gold studs. The King hadn't even used it yet. Today would be the first time.

'Sir Percival!' came a soft, hissing voice.

A sinister figure in a long, black furred gown glided out of the shadows. It was Dr Septimus Slide, the King's physician. Toby shivered. Of all the plotters in the palace, he feared Dr Slide the most. He was always spying, whispering, scheming. People said he practised alchemy and the dark arts. And he certainly seemed to have the sick old King in his power. Often, he was the only one the King allowed in his bedchamber.

Apart from Sir Percival Plopping of course. The Groom of the Stool was always allowed in. But not any more, it seemed. Dr Slide thrust out a bony hand. 'I'll have that key,' he said. 'I will attend to the King on his new close stool.'

'Begone, thou spider, thou creeping toad, thou creature of the night!' thundered Sir Percival, hanging the key round his neck to keep it safe. Then his eyes widened. 'You have the King's ring on your finger!' he roared.

'Yea, he was pleased to give it me,' said Dr Slide, flashing the silver ring, with its enormous ruby, about. 'A present to his most loyal, humble servant.'

Sir Percival's face flushed a deep, angry red. 'Devil take you!' he growled.

The creepy physician could make the King do anything he wanted. And he could see the King any time he liked. Dr Slide lived in lodgings right at the top of the palace. And his rooms had a private staircase, which only he used, that led directly to the King's bedchamber.'

'Give me that key,' insisted Dr Slide again.

'Step aside or I will break your head!' was Sir Percival's reply.

Dr Slide shrivelled into a corner, his eyes flickering like a lizard.

'See, Toby,' boomed Sir Percival. 'See how his eyes whirl about? How can such a man be trusted?' And with a snort of disgust – '*Pah!*' – he strode through another door in the outer chamber. It was a magnificent oak door, carved with lions, and it led to the King's apartments.

In moments he was back again. 'I forgot the King's licorice lozenges.' When the King was in a temper, feeding him sweeties could sometimes soothe him. Sir Percival grabbed a box from the table and dashed off again.

Toby was alone now with Dr Slide. The Keeper of the Key of the King's Close Stool could feel his legs shaking. Sir Percival was a fearless, honest knight. There wasn't a scheming bone in his body. But Toby wished he wouldn't talk like that to the King's physician. He didn't seem to realize how dangerous Dr Slide could be. Sir Percival had only had this job a few weeks. The last Groom of the Stool, Sir Thomas Heneage, had been sacked in mysterious circumstances and the whisper round the palace was that it was all Dr Slide's doing.

Dr Slide stroked his long, white forked beard. His eyes blazed hatred at the door through which Sir Percival had disappeared. Than he turned his cobra-like stare on Toby. Toby felt himself shrinking inside, his head spinning. It must be true that this man had magic powers.

'Sir Percival is pleased to treat me with contempt,' said the doctor in a menacing whisper. 'But he is a clown, a simple-minded clod, with a head as soft as a baked apple. He is no match for Dr Septimus Slide. And, mark my words, he will rue the day he ever mocked me.'

He slithered back through the carved oak door into the King's private apartments. But his evil presence seemed to linger in the room like a dark cloud.

Toby waited, alone in the outer chamber. From the maze of secret rooms beyond the door, he heard a thin, peevish voice. It was King Henry having a tantrum. Toby had often heard the King ranting and raving. He'd seen huge meals going in for him: stewed sparrows, jellies and his favourite orange pies. But he'd never seen the King himself. He'd never been allowed beyond that great oak door.

He'd sometimes ask Sir Percival, 'What is it like, beyond the door?'

But Sir Percival wasn't good at describing things. Occasionally, he'd say, 'His Majesty's bad leg pains him today.' But that was all.

A whiskery face peeped out of Toby's doublet. It was Toby's pet, Roger, the sewer rat. He wasn't grey like the other sewer rats. He was something special: a rare albino rat, with white fur and red eyes that glowed like rubies. Toby had found him down in the drains. He'd rescued Roger from the savage grey sewer rats, who attacked him because he looked different.

And what had Toby been doing down in those drains with the sewer rats? He'd been raking poo off the walls. Drain-raking was Toby's first job, after his parents died of the plague. With a gang of other kids, he'd gone round the royal palaces in turn, cleaning the drains that ran from the privies to the Thames. It was filthy, disgusting work.

But Sir Percival had changed all that. That's

why he was Toby's hero. Just a few weeks ago, when Toby was cleaning the drains under Whitehall Palace, Roger had escaped. He'd scampered up into a palace privy, with Toby climbing after him. Unfortunately, Sir Percival was sitting on the privy at the time. He'd shot off it like a rocket. And Toby had thought, *I'm done for.* Other gentlemen would have had him flogged or even executed as a spy.

But was the good knight angry when a rat and a drain-raker came out of his privy? Not Sir Percival. He'd just roared with laughter, slapping his long leather boots. 'By my troth, boy!' he'd bellowed. 'You gave me a turn. But what is that foul stink? It is you? Methinks you need some sweet-smelling perfume!'

And, to Toby's amazement, Sir Percival hadn't sent him back down the drains or had him punished. Instead, the good knight had been kind to him, brought him fine clothes, found him a job as the Keeper of the Key of the King's Close Stool. Already Toby loved the bluff old knight like a father.

A fresh racket came from beyond the door. Toby snapped out of his daydream.

Dr Slide was screeching, 'Help! Treason! Murder!'

Suddenly, Sir Percival came bursting from the King's private rooms, pursued by two of the King's bodyguard armed with poleaxes. 'Dr Slide says I have poisoned the King!' he roared at Toby.

Through the other door came crashing the Sergeant at Arms with a whole squad of armed men. Sir Percival was surrounded.

Then, from the King's rooms, Dr Slide came slinking out. He was carrying two glass flasks. Dr Slide often had glass flasks. He used them to study the King's pee and diagnose what was wrong with him. But today, the royal pee looked very scary. In one flask it was bright blue, in the other green and fizzy.

'See!' cried Dr Slide, holding up the flasks triumphantly. 'The King's pee shows clear proof of poison!' He pointed a finger, with a nail so long it curled back upon itself like a pig's tail. 'And I suspect it is in the licorice lozenges which Sir Percival gives him! By God's grace, I have discovered this plot in time. I have given the King medicines to cure him.'

Sir Percival struggled in his captors' grip. 'He lies! The treacherous villain! It is *he* who means the King harm!'

And Toby, his heart pounding, tried to help.

'Sir Percival is no poisoner!' he protested. But Dr Slide turned on him, with those cobra eyes glittering. 'I fear there is witchcraft here!' he said in that menacing hiss.

'What do you mean?' asked the Sergeant at Arms. But already his soldiers were muttering in fear.

'See for yourselves,' said Dr Slide. He pointed a long, yellow curly nail at Toby. 'The boy has a familiar.'

The men muttered even more. Everyone knew that witches had familiars. Creatures who attended them, like hares or cats – or rats. And, at that very moment, Roger poked his nose out of Toby's doublet, as if he too was hypnotized by Dr Slide's stare.

'The boy is part of the plot too! Take them both to the Tower!' howled Dr Slide. 'Put them to torture!'

Soldiers grappled with Sir Percival. Some leapt forward to seize Toby. From out of the scrum of soldiers came Sir Percival's desperate cry: 'Save yourself, boy. Run for your life!'

Toby ran. He raced through the great halls, courtyards and long galleries of the palace. Up and down stairs he sped, through hot, greasy kitchens and dark passages, not daring to look behind him. He stumbled into the overgrown tilt-yard where the King had once jousted.

He rested, breathless, behind some tall purple weeds. Every second he expected a hand on his shoulder: 'I arrest you, for plotting the King's murder!' But no armed men came clattering after him. Maybe they hadn't even followed him.

Toby should have taken the good knight's advice. He should have run far away from Whitehall. But he didn't. Instead, he crept down to the river. Lurking in shadows, he watched Sir Percival being dragged out of the palace by armed men, protesting his innocence every step of the way.

'I am falsely accused! Dr Slide lies! Break into his lodgings. There you will find evidence against him!' No one listened. No one spoke up for him. They were all too scared of Dr Slide.

Toby looked up at Dr Slide's lodgings, right at the top of the palace. No one knew what the doctor did up there. He was sometimes seen on the roof, especially in storms, like a great bat, with his cloak billowing around him.

'He is a wizard,' the servants would whisper. 'He commands the thunder. He rules the lightning.' Behind his back, they called him Storm Master.

As Toby gazed upward, his heart almost stopped. Was that the old Storm Master himself, gazing down? 'You must leave, NOW,' he told himself. There was nothing he could do to help Sir Percival. He was being rowed off to the Tower in a boat crammed with armed soldiers. Most people who went in there never came out, except to have their heads chopped off. Sir Percival would see some of those heads on spikes as he passed under London Bridge.

Toby clenched his fists in fury at his own helplessness. At the same time, tears stung his eyes. 'I *will* prove his innocence,' he whispered. 'I will find the evidence Sir Percival spoke of.' Even if it meant sneaking back into Whitehall and searching Dr Slide's lodgings. But how would Toby reach them? The only way was through the King's bedchamber. The very thought of such a perilous journey made him tremble. And even if he found the evidence, what then?

'I shall show His Majesty himself!' Toby decided desperately. 'I shall beg for Sir Percival's life!' The thought made him tremble even more. Toby had never even seen the King, just heard him roaring in his rooms, like a great angry bear in its cave.

'Oi, you there!'

Toby whirled round. Oh no, armed men! Dr Slide must have seen him from that high window and called the guard. He took off and this time he really was running for his life.

# CHAPTER FIVE

'I'll have to have a rethink,' quacked Superloo, who wasn't the least down-hearted at landing in the wrong place. It had no doubt its giant computer brain would come up with another plan. 'But I need to know where we are. Go out and have a scout around.'

'I told you, it's scary out there,' Finn replied. 'It's not the kind of neighbourhood where a king would live.'

'On the contrary,' said Superloo, who always knew better. 'In Tudor London, slums were often right next to palace walls. Just go to the end of the alley,' it coaxed. 'I'm certain my calculations aren't far out. I bet Whitehall is only a few steps away.'

Finn sighed. As usual, the toilet made it sound easy. But it wasn't the one taking the risk. On the other hand, Finn knew he didn't have much choice. Now Superloo was back in Tudor times, it wouldn't go home without its toilet relative.

'All right, let's get this over with,' said Finn. 'But I'm not going far.' He straightened his floppy cowpat cap in Superloo's mirror. 'I look like a prat. Are you sure everyone wore these?'

'Of course!' said the toilet. 'They were really cool in Tudor times. But don't forget, you're a peasant. Take your hat off and bow to anyone posher than you. That's almost everyone,' it added. 'And remember there's lots of rules in Tudor times. Especially for poor people. They couldn't play skittles, cards or dice. They couldn't wear fur, silk, gold or scarlet. They couldn't say anything rude about the King . . .'

'Yeah, yeah, I know,' said Finn. 'Or they got their heads chopped off.'

'Actually,' said the toilet airily, 'that was usually reserved for lords and ladies. The poor had a much crueller death called hanging, drawing and quartering.'

'Spare me the details!' begged Finn, whose stomach was already churning. 'I'm going, OK?'

'Watch yourself out there,' said Superloo as Finn poked his nose out of the cubicle door. And Finn knew that, despite all its faults – its selfishness, its scheming and its giant ego – the toilet really did care about him. They'd been a team now on quite a few rescue missions.

'I'll be careful,' Finn answered gravely as he stepped outside.

He ducked round the cart and checked up and down the dark, stinking alley. His feet were in something squelchy. What was that scuffling in the shadows? Finn's heart beat faster. 'There's nobody here,' he reassured himself. It was probably only a rat. He took a deep breath and began to creep along the alley.

As soon as Finn had gone, two boys came out from behind a dunghill They were thieves – quick-witted, nimble rascals always on the lookout to make a dishonest penny.

They worked together. Jago was the tickler, Snip the cutpurse. They'd choose their prey – maybe a rich young lord with a fat purse hanging from his belt. But people kept a hand on their purses in London – there were thieves about! So Jago would slip up behind the young lord and tickle his ear with a straw. The man would put his hand up to scratch and, like lightning, Snip was in there with his sharp little knife, slicing off the purse. The young lord would swagger off, not realizing he'd been robbed. Not until he felt for his purse again. Then he'd yell for a constable: 'Help, ho! Cutpurse!' He'd draw his sword to skewer the villains. But by then Snip and Jago would have melted into the crowd.

'Snip, my good rogue, what have we here?' asked Jago. They circled Superloo's shiny walls. The cubicle door was still open a crack. Snip put his eye to the gap.

'By my cuttle-bung!' he cried, reeling back in amazement. ''Tis a privy! A silver privy. Fit for a king!'

Superloo knew full well they were there. It had heard them coming and was eavesdropping on their conversation. It didn't think it was in any danger. Besides, it was too busy being scholarly, searching through the data in its giant computer brain.

*Ahhh,* cuttle-bung, it was thinking. *I believe that is Tudor slang.* Cuttle *means knife.* Bung *means purse. Hence* cuttle-bung, *a cutpurse's knife! How very authentic and colourful.*

It should have taught Finn some Tudor

slang. It would have helped him blend in better. 'Never mind,' the toilet genius consoled itself. It was a big responsibility planning these rescue missions. You couldn't think of every little thing.

'Methinks it is the King's,' said Jago. 'Who left it here, I wonder?'

'I care not about that,' said Snip. 'We be lifters both. Let's lift it.' He was already heaving at the old hay cart, struggling to free its wheels from the mud. 'We have need of a prancer or two,' he grumbled as he puffed and panted.

'*Prancers*,' mused the toilet, its brain whirring. 'Let's see. That's Tudor slang for horses. And *lifters*? That's obvious. *Lifters* are thieves, so *to lift* means . . . *Aaaargh!*'

The toilet felt itself being tipped. Jago pushed it over while Snip, using all his strength, pushed the cart underneath. *Whump!* Superloo crashed on to the cart. There was a muffled squawk from inside, half-drowned by a drunken song from The Spotted Pig.

'Did you hear someone cry out close by?' said Snip, gazing nervously up and down the alley.

'Not I.' Jago shook his head. 'I heard nothing but the roar from the alehouse.'

'Then let us be off right quick with this privy,' said Snip.

'To what place?' asked Jago.

'I have a plan,' said Snip, his cunning little eyes glittering in the gloom.

They each took a shaft of the old cart. Cursing at what hard work it was, they dragged Superloo off, between the wonky, half-toppling houses, in the opposite direction to the one Finn had taken.

Finn had no idea that Superloo was being kidnapped. He had serious problems of his own. He'd only meant to go to the end of the alley – to see if Whitehall Palace was nearby. But the alley was longer and twistier than he thought. At last he saw a patch of brightness.

*The end of the alley*, he thought. *About time.* It was daylight out there! It was so dark down the alley, he'd supposed they'd landed at night. He stepped out on to the street, blinking in the winter sun.

At once, Finn was caught up in a crush of people. Noise battered his ears. Shouts came from everywhere, 'Chimney sweep, mistress!' 'Buy my fine oysters!' He dodged a lurching waggon pulled by steaming horses, then tripped over a scavenging dog. Hurrying people barged into him, jostled him about.

'Watch out below!'

Finn gazed upwards, his mouth open. A woman leaned over her window sill with a brimming chamber pot.

*Oh no!* thought Finn, leaping aside as its contents splashed down.

'Let me pass, wretch!' A man in fine scarlet robes trimmed with fur kicked him out of the way, like a stray dog.

Finn scooped his hat from the mud and gazed round in panic. Where was he? Where was Whitehall? But he had no time to find out.

'Clubs!' came a furious yell. ''Prentices to me! Clubs! Clubs!'

*What's going on?* thought Finn, bewildered. The citizens scattered. Tudor women picked up their skirts and fled. Mothers hustled their children to safety. Then Finn saw a mob of boys surge down the street. They knocked down a market stall. Apples rolled everywhere; chickens fluttered away squawking.

Finn should have moved faster. One second he was standing there, dazed and confused.

The next, he was plunged into a street battle. Finn didn't know it, but the Carpenters were fighting the Fishmongers. A Fishmonger's apprentice had slapped a Carpenter's lad with a wet turbot. The cry 'Clubs!' had gone up and now there was a full-scale riot.

But then another cry went up: 'Constables!' The street emptied for the second time and the apprentices scattered, quick as cockroaches, darting down alleyways and disappearing.

Tough men in leather jerkins, armed with staffs, came running into the street. *The police!* thought Finn.

'There be one of those 'prentice wretches!' cried a barber-surgeon, peering from a doorway in his bloodstained apron.

'As I be an honest citizen, he was in the thick of it,' a housewife agreed, leaning from her upstairs window.

Finn's brain told him, 'Run!'

'Where be you off to in such hot haste?' growled a voice right by his ear. A brawny arm picked him up by the scruff of his neck and shook him like a dog shakes a rabbit. A bristly face, with hot, stinking breath, was thrust into his own.

'I wasn't with them,' Finn began to babble.

'I was just walking along, minding my own business –'

'Hold your peace!' snarled the constable. 'Your hair betrays you. You be a 'prentice boy – or I'm a Dutchman!'

*My hair?* thought Finn. *What's my hair got to do with it?* And where were they taking him? He was being frogmarched to the shop of the barber-surgeon.

'Let me go!' shrieked Finn, struggling like mad. He'd heard about barber-surgeons. They pulled out rotten teeth and chopped legs off with no anaesthetic.

He was forced to sit on an upturned barrel. The barber-surgeon picked up some wicked-looking iron shears.

'Help!' shrieked Finn as the man approached in his bloody apron. What terrible Tudor punishment was this? But Finn couldn't move. The constables had him pinned down.

Then something heavy was plonked on his head. Was it some fiendish torture machine? No. It was a pudding basin. But still Finn was quaking. He could hear the sound of chopping shears. But he couldn't see a thing – the pudding basin covered his eyes. Suddenly, the basin was whipped off and Finn stared around in panic. Then he saw his hair lying on the floor. He reached a shaking hand up to his head.

*They've given me a haircut*, he thought, bewildered. His hair had been lopped off all round, just above his ears where the pudding basin had come to.

'Can I go now, please?' begged Finn. The alley where Superloo was waiting wasn't far. He could practically see it from where he was sitting. He longed to run back to the safety of that silver cubicle. But they hadn't finished with him yet. The constables seized him again and hustled him out of the shop.

Another brawling bunch of apprentices came roaring down the street. There were fists flying, feet kicking, even head-whacking with cudgels! But this time the constables didn't arrest them. Instead, they smiled indulgently.

''Prentices ever love a jolly game of football,' said one.

Then Finn saw a pig's bladder ball soaring into the air. Someone had given it a mighty boot. *That's a girl!* thought Finn.

A girl with long ginger curls fought her way free of the scrum and hared after the ball she'd just kicked. She picked it up and ran like mad.

She was trying to reach the goal, which was some distance away. The others went whooping after her.

'Did you see that red-haired young wench,' asked one constable, 'who gave the ball such a goodly wallop? Is she not 'prentice to Mrs Harris? Is she not forbidden to play football?'

'Aye,' grinned the other. 'And Mrs Harris will be madder than a baited bear when she finds out.'

Questions were buzzing in Finn's brain too. A girl apprentice? He didn't know they were allowed. And one good at football? Finn thought Tudor girls stayed indoors and made tapestries and played the lute. And did Tudor football actually have any rules? To Finn, it didn't look much different from the street fight he'd seen before. But there was no time to puzzle over any of this. Now the game had moved on, the constables marched Finn off again.

'Where are we going?' cried Finn. Not far as it turned out. Along the street was a little market square. And in the middle of the square were – *Stocks!* thought Finn, panicking all over again. He should have known he wouldn't escape with just a haircut.

They were double stocks, for two criminals. And someone was already in them. It was a boy about Finn's age. A jeering crowd of children surrounded him. A girl picked up a handful of horse dung and pelted him with it. It splattered all over his face. The children cheered and screamed with laughter.

'Good shot, Bess!' one shouted.

Finn struggled wildly. 'I'm not going in there! I haven't done anything!' But it was no use. The burly constables held him fast.

One growled, 'Be still, boy, or you shall get a beating.' They chased off the mocking crowd and forced Finn to sit down on some filthy straw. They lifted the top wooden bar, shoved his legs inside, then clamped it down again.

Finn stared at his legs inside the stock sandwich and wondered, 'How did I get myself into this mess?'

# CHAPTER SIX

Sunk in his own misery, Finn hardly noticed the dung-spattered boy beside him in the stocks. Until he spoke.

'My name is Toby,' he said. 'How came you here?'

Finn frowned. He had no idea really. And out of the corner of his eye, he could see those kids creeping back again, armed with rotten, stinking cabbage leaves.

'They said I was a 'prentice or something,' he told Toby.

'They said that of me also,' said Toby. 'It was ill luck. But it has been a day of ill luck for me.'

And he told his neighbour in the stocks what had happened, about how Sir Percival had been wrongly accused and arrested. How, chased by armed men, he'd run in a blind panic through the streets, not even sure where he was going. He'd lost them at last. But then, like Finn, he'd been caught up in that wild mob of fighting apprentices. Constables had collared him, said, 'You wretch, did you steal that silk doublet? It is far too fine for a fishmonger's 'prentice!' They'd stuck him in the stocks until he confessed the truth.

But how could he tell them, 'I am Keeper of the Key of the King's Close Stool. Sir Percival gave me this doublet'? That would reveal who he really was. He'd be dragged off to the Tower too, clapped in chains in a stinking dungeon.

Finn listened while Toby poured out his story. It was clear to Finn that Toby was just as scared and distressed as he was. But apart from that, he couldn't grasp much. Was Toby speaking English? Like the constables, some of his words made sense. Something about Sir Percival Plopping being in peril of his life. But other words just sounded like gibberish.

'Look,' said Finn when Toby had finished. 'I didn't get much of that. But my name's Finn, right? And I've got to get out of here!' A rotting cabbage leaf struck him in the mouth. He spat it out miserably. He was shivering now in his coal-sack costume. There was no warmth in that winter sun and the cold was creeping through to his bones.

Toby was wiping slimy rotten egg off his face. He could hardly understand Finn either. He thought he must be a foreigner who couldn't speak English properly. But there was no doubt they agreed about one thing. 'I must escape too,' said Toby. 'And right quick!'

But how could they? A constable had been left on guard so they didn't get away. And there were honest citizens about who would catch them if they tried to flee.

'Duck!' cried Finn as a respectable-looking old lady lobbed a lump of horse dung.

'Villains!' she cried. 'You should be hung, drawn and quartered!'

Then Roger poked his whiskery face out of Toby's doublet. The faithful rat had clung on as his master had raced madly through the streets. Now he came out and perched on Toby's shoulder.

'Is that your rat?' said Finn, shrinking away. But he could hardly object. The rat was much cleaner than he was. It sat grooming itself in the sunshine, cleaning its silky white coat.

The guard, who'd been looking bored, ambled over.

'What is that strange beast?' he demanded. Like most Tudor folk, he'd never seen a pure white rat like Roger.

Suddenly, Toby had a brainwave. 'If it please you, constable, it is the Queen's rat,' he said.

The constable furrowed his brow. He was a bit slow on the uptake but he finally twigged. 'Our queen?' he asked excitedly. He had to think for a moment who was queen now – it was hard to keep up with Henry's wives. 'I know, 'tis Katharine Parr! They say she has a spaniel, Rig. He has a gold collar! But I never heard tell of a rat.' On the other hand, he could see this was no ordinary rat. It was a very fine rat, a noble rat, a rat fit for a queen.

'How came you by Her Majesty's rat?' he demanded.

Toby hung his head and looked guilty. 'I stole him,' he mumbled. 'And I am most heartily sorry for it now. I wish there was a way to return him.'

'Would there be a goodly reward,' asked the constable, 'for returning the Queen's rat?'

'They say the Queen dotes on him,' said Toby, keeping his head low so the constable couldn't see the spark of hope in his eyes. 'Even more than her spaniel, Rig. She would gladly give a purse of silver.'

'Do you think so?' marvelled the constable.

'Or even gold,' suggested Toby.

The constable's eyes glittered greedily. 'Begone!' he ordered the crowd of dung-throwing citizens. He wanted that reward all to himself. He stomped forward to snatch Roger off Toby's shoulder. But suddenly, Roger whisked back inside his master's doublet. The constable lunged again as Roger's pink nose poked out at Toby's neck, his cuffs and through the fashionable slashes in his hose.

'Curse that rat!' cried the constable. 'Will he not stay still!'

'I beseech you, good constable,' said Toby humbly. 'Set me free for a moment and I will catch him for you.' Finn had been looking on, confused. He couldn't fathom this rat business. What on earth was Toby up to?

The constable hesitated, but only for a second – that reward was too tempting. And Toby seemed like a decent lad, who repented of his crime. So he opened the stocks. Toby stood up, wincing at the cramp in his legs. He felt inside his doublet and brought Roger out, sitting on his hand.

The constable put down his poleaxe. He grabbed for Roger with both hands. There was no way he was letting this rat escape. It meant riches to him, more gold than he'd ever dreamed of.

Toby shouted, 'Flee, Finn!'

Finn had only just realized – lifting that bar had freed his legs too. And he didn't need telling twice. He dashed away. Behind him he heard a yell. Roger had nipped the constable with his needle-sharp teeth. He took a flying leap and landed on Toby's shoulder.

'Seize them!' bawled the constable. Finn skidded to a halt and looked back. Toby was staggering behind, his legs wobbly as jelly – he'd been stuck in those stocks much longer than Finn. Finn raced back and grabbed him, dragging him along. All they had to do was reach Superloo's cubicle.

Together, they squeezed into the narrow gap between houses. Sploshed through evil-smelling sludge. Shivering, they hid in the shadows. But the hue and cry passed by. The constable and his posse of citizens missed the alley entrance completely and went haring off down the street.

Finn scuttled on down the alley, Toby stumbling behind him. Suddenly, Finn stopped and stared about. Had he got it wrong? No, down there was The Spotted Pig . And this was the place where Superloo had landed. Just beside the wattle and daub wall with the flaky blue paint. Only Superloo wasn't here.

In a panic, Finn raced up and down, even though he knew Superloo couldn't move without help. Unless, of course, it had gone back to the twenty-first century. Finn was really panicking now. He felt sick.

*It wouldn't*, he thought. It wouldn't just abandon him in Tudor times. Would it? You never quite knew the way that toilet's brain worked. It had its own agenda. It had often promised never to leave Finn in the past. But could you believe it?

'That lying toilet,' Finn spat out, almost in tears, as Toby stood bewildered beside him. 'Why did I ever trust it? It's gone back home without me!'

# CHAPTER SEVEN

**B**ack in the twenty-first century, Hans Dryer had reached his destination – the small northern town where Finn lived and where Hi-Tech Toilets was located. At that very moment, he was sitting in his small, cell-like hotel room. It was beige, featureless and instantly forgettable. Just like him.

But to judge Mr Hans Dryer by his appearance would have been a big mistake. In the inside pocket of his grey suit there was a business card. It said simply:

**ROBOT HUNTERS INC.**

*Problems with your Bot?*
*Give us a call!*
*We locate. We terminate.*

Mr Hans Dryer was a hired assassin. He would work for any government, any organization. You just had to pay his bosses enough. But he didn't terminate people – he killed *machines*, uppity robots who had broken free of human control. And he didn't need guns or any hi-tech military gear. His only weapon was the laptop computer he carried in that slim black briefcase.

Mr Hans Dryer opened up his laptop and switched it on. He'd dealt with lots of rogue robots. There were more of them around than people realized. But news of them was always hushed up, for fear of causing a panic. You could imagine the headlines:

### 'CRAZY BOTS OUT OF CONTROL!' 'MAD MACHINES TAKE OVER THE WORLD!'

The Care Bots, who'd taken over that old people's home? Mr Hans Dryer had been called in there. And the Wheelie Bin Bots who were supposed to wheel themselves out for the bin men, but who'd ended up chasing them down the street, snapping their lids like hungry crocs? Mr Hans Dryer had dealt with them, no problem.

Soon, he'd even be sent into space. It had all been kept secret – but there were rogue bots on the moon. They'd been landed from an unmanned space rocket. They were supposed to trundle about picking up moon-rock samples, but they'd run away and set up their own little colony in a crater.

But the Space Bots were second on his hit list. First he had to find and terminate Superloo and retrieve that four-billion-dollar microchip.

'Now to start setting my trap,' said Mr Hans Dryer to himself in that strange, expressionless voice. The reason he was the best in the business was that he was so good at reading the robot mind. These super-brainy machines thought they were invincible, but, just like people, they had their weaknesses.

His pale eyes glittered briefly. Mr Hans Dryer never showed any emotion; he was always 100 per cent professional. But secretly, he really enjoyed his job. That's because he hated robots. He thought they were freaks – metal monstrosities who didn't deserve to live.

He'd never encountered one like Superloo

before. Did it even classify as a robot? Mr Hans Dryer thought so. It was just a machine like all the rest, a computer brain inside a tin-can body. This one was supposed to be extra-intelligent. But that didn't bother Mr Hans Dryer a bit because he had a plan. With his uncanny skills, he'd already guessed what made Superloo vulnerable – its vanity and its loneliness.

He began typing. Words appeared on his glowing computer screen. He'd already set up a fake website – an on-line dating agency called *Lonely Loos*. And now he was pretending to be a ladies' toilet, looking for love.

'I am a super-intelligent, ladies-only public convenience,' Hans Dryer wrote, 'with no-touch flushing and automatic self-cleaning. Is there anybody out there like ME? Are YOU a lonely toilet genius? If you are, I'm dying to meet you, for fun times and possible long-term relationship. GSOH essential.'

# CHAPTER EIGHT

Finn was plunged into total despair. He could still hardly believe that Superloo had gone home without him. Then he noticed something. 'The cart's not here either,' he muttered.

It had been dragged away. You could see deep wheel ruts in the mud. Then, further along the alley, Finn saw something else. He squinted into the gloom. Shining white on the mud was a single square of white toilet paper. Then he saw another and another, leading off down the alley. He turned to Toby with a shout of delight.

'Hey, look! Superloo hasn't gone back to the twenty-first century. It went somewhere on a cart. And, look, it's left a trail. Come on!'

Toby hung back. 'I have urgent business at Whitehall.'

'The palace, you mean?' said Finn. 'Then stay with me. Cos I bet that's where Superloo's going!' He could see it all now. The wily toilet, sick of waiting and anxious to rescue its relative, had probably persuaded some humans to take it where it wanted to go.

'Just follow the toilet-paper trail,' said Finn, 'and I bet you anything it'll lead to the palace.'

Toby followed reluctantly. He was making some kind of protest. But Finn couldn't wait to listen to that. He was desperate to catch up with Superloo. That toilet was his ride home, his only way back to the twenty-first century. He dashed off.

Finn didn't know it, but Superloo wasn't going to Whitehall. Snip and Jago had other plans.

Superloo felt itself being jogged along on the cart. Its sensors told it they were out of alleyways now and on busy streets. It closed its cubicle door for its own protection. That meant it couldn't leave any more toilet paper for Finn to follow. Not that that mattered much. Its trail would only be trampled underfoot by the crowds. They seemed to be in an excited holiday mood. They were heading in the same direction as the cart. But where to?

A constant stream of complaints and commands came from inside the cubicle. 'This is no way to treat a toilet genius!' And, 'Take me to Whitehall Palace immediately!' But no one could hear it above the din.

At last, the cart stopped. Superloo felt itself being slid off. With a jarring thump it stood upright. *About time*, it thought. It didn't appreciate being tipped on its side and transported on some clapped-out, creaky old hay cart. It was so undignified.

'These ignorant humans,' it huffed to itself. 'They don't know who they're dealing with.' It opened its door a few centimetres. '*Hummm. Now where am I?*'

A muddle of smells wafted in on the breeze. Superloo's microchip brain was fitted with many special features. And one of these was an Electronic Nose. It was a sophisticated little device, smaller than a pinhead, designed to test the air quality in spaceships. But it was also dead useful for identifying Tudor pongs. The E-nose got busy analysing.

'I detect,' murmured Superloo, 'the sweaty armpits of people who never take baths. And the perfume they use to cover their stink.

And greasy, roasting pork. And warm ginger-bread and hot chestnuts.'

Its sensors were picking up sounds too: tootling pipes, twanging lutes, warbling ballad singers, the *chink, chink, chink* of money constantly changing hands. Superloo fed all this data into its brilliant computer brain. Which came up with an answer in 2.5 seconds.

'I'm at a Tudor fair!' Superloo quacked in annoyance. There were loads of them in London, especially on public holidays.

A cry outside confirmed it. 'Buy my ginger-bread, good mistress, the finest at the fair!'

'But I wanted to be at Whitehall!' Superloo fretted. Then another voice made it forget about that. It was very close, just outside the cubicle.

'Here be wonders!' Snip was bawling. 'Good people, draw near! Here is the King's very own privy! One penny to go inside. Better than the bull with five legs, better than the dancing hare. Truly this is a miracle!'

Snip stopped yelling and Jago whispered, 'Here they come. Fools fresh from the country. See how they gape and stare! Be ready to take their money, good Snip.'

'And there is not even need for my cuttle-bung,' Snip sniggered.

*I'm being put on display!* thought Superloo, shocked beyond belief. *For money! Me, Superloo, the most highly evolved, super-intelligent toilet ever. As if I were some kind of freak! Like a three-headed sheep or something!* Its cubicle practically shook with outrage. It was going to slam its door shut to keep out the gawping mob when Snip roared out again.

'Masters all, this privy is marvellous to behold. It is a noble privy, a *prince* among privies.'

*That's more like it*, thought Superloo, calming down a bit.

'It is the finest privy in all the world,' Snip continued. 'Be respectful, my good sirs; take off your caps when you enter here.'

*These Tudors really know how to treat a toilet*, thought Superloo, forgetting its bad mood and sliding its door open a bit wider.

The punters shuffled in, filling the tiny cubicle. They were simple country people, come up to London for a day out. Superloo heard their cries of wonder, '*Ohhhh!*' '*Ahhhh!*' 'See how it sparkles!' Superloo flushed its toilet bowl once, twice. The cries of wonder grew even louder.

'This be something to tell my grand-children!' said one peasant woman. 'That once, I saw the King's privy!' She gave a great sigh as if now she could die happy.

The world's brainiest toilet was really enjoying itself. It just loved being the centre of attention. And it was certainly causing a big sensation. It showed off a bit more by making its bog roll swivel. '*Ooooo!*' everyone cried, even more amazed than before.

But suddenly, there was a commotion outside. A stern voice barked, 'How came you by this privy?' The peasants inside Superloo melted away. They knew an official's voice when they heard it. It was the Steward of the Fair, backed up by some constables.

'Seize the rogues!' he cried as Snip and Jago tried to run.

Finn and Toby had come to the end of the toilet-paper trail.

'Where do we go now?' asked Finn, baffled. 'Is Whitehall near?'

Toby shook his head. That's what he'd been trying to tell Finn. They'd been going in the wrong direction. 'Whitehall is that way,' he said, pointing down the street.

*So where is Superloo going?* thought Finn, staring around.

A boy came out of a printer's shop and nailed up a poster. It was hot from the press, with the ink still wet. Finn jostled with a crowd of people, trying to see. It had obviously been printed in a big hurry. There was a crude picture of some box-like thing, with a jumble of strange, spiky letters underneath.

'What's it say?' he begged Toby.

Toby frowned. 'I cannot read.' Sir Percival had promised to teach him but they'd never had time.

'Wait a minute,' said Finn as some words finally made sense. 'It says *King* and *Privie*. Hey, that picture, I think it's of Superloo!' He scanned the poster again and made out another word. 'It says *Fayre*,' he told Toby excitedly. 'Is there a fair around here? Is that where all these people are going?'

Toby had no time to reply. Finn grabbed his arm and they were swept along in the throng.

'Let me go!' said Toby, shaking himself free. 'I must get to Whitehall!' But by then they were among the stalls. Finn saw a glinting silver roof in the distance.

'It's Superloo!' he cried and rushed off towards it.

'Wait!' commanded Toby. Now it was his turn to grab Finn's arms. He could see constables – that meant trouble. But worse than that, a squad of armed men came clanking up. They were the King's own men, his Yeomen of the Guard in scarlet tunics and silver breastplates. What were they doing here? Officials were running about like headless chickens.

One was ranting, 'His Grace's privy must be returned to Whitehall! It be treason to steal the King's privy. And treason twice over to let such country clods gaze upon it!' Snip gulped hard and Jago was already shivering. They both knew the terrible punishment for treason. But they were in the grip of a burly constable.

'We meant no harm,' snivelled Jago.

'We did not lift it,' sobbed Snip. 'We came across it by chance.'

The constable laughed. He'd heard that excuse before.

As Finn and Toby watched, Superloo was hoisted on to the shoulders of eight Yeomen. In solemn procession, they carried it away through the streets. One walked in front to clear the crowds. 'Make way for the King's privy!'

*The King's privy?* thought Toby, confused. *Stolen?* He'd never seen a privy like that in any of the King's palaces. And anyway, these days, Henry only used close stools. The royal bum preferred soft padded seats.

'I've got to follow that privy!' gabbled Finn. He tried to push his way through the crowds but already he'd lost sight of Superloo.

'They are taking it to Whitehall,' said Toby. 'And that's where I am bound.'

'Great!' said Finn. 'Can I come with you?'

'With all my heart,' said Toby. 'But we must hurry. Time is wasting!' The sooner he found that evidence the better. Sir Percival could be led to the scaffold as soon as dawn tomorrow. Dr Slide would make sure there was the least possible delay. The two boys dashed off, with Toby leading the way.

Back at the fair, the constable growled, 'What do I do with these two villains?' He had Jago by the scruff of the neck in one hand, Snip in the other. He lifted both boys high off the ground and started to shake them.

'It's jail for them,' said the Steward, 'there to await justice!'

Suddenly, the constable dropped Jago as if he was red-hot and started madly scratching his ear. Snip saw his chance and wriggled free. Both boys ran like hares. There was a hue and cry behind them but they were too fast for the lumbering constables. They ran down to the Thames, to one of their many secret dens. This one was beneath a rotten old rowing boat, dumped upside down on a mudbank.

Safe in the dark, under the boat, Jago said, 'I had high hopes, when we happened upon the King's privy. I thought, "We shall be rich. I shall buy me some new duds and stampers. Maybe even a prancer!"'

If Superloo had been listening, it would have been thrilled to hear more Tudor slang. 'Ah, *stampers* and *duds*,' it would have said, whizzing through its vast data banks. 'That means shoes and clothes.'

'But those constables took all our money. We have not even a penny,' Jago continued mournfully. 'We shall go hungry tonight.'

'Be of good cheer,' Snip told his partner. 'We shall eat right well tonight.' And he took a little leather purse out of his tunic. He shook it so the coins jingled inside.

'How came you by that?' asked Jago, amazed.

'From the constable,' said Snip. 'When you tickled his ear with your straw, I lifted his purse with my little cuttle-bung!'

# CHAPTER NINE

Superloo was having a whale of a time. It was being taken up the Thames to Whitehall in *The Lyon*, Henry's magnificent royal barge. The world's cleverest toilet reclined on cushions under a canopy of cloth of gold, while rowers sweated away at the oars.

Smaller boats rowed alongside to accompany the toilet. They were crammed with nobles and important officials. In one was the Mayor of London, wearing red robes and a golden chain. In another musicians played on lutes and sang ballads in praise of Superloo. Crowds of swans came gliding up, as if they too wanted to see the famous toilet.

Citizens lined the riverbank. As the procession passed, they tossed their caps in the air and cheered.

*Wow! They love me!* thought Superloo, tickled pink. This was even better than the fair.

Word had spread like wildfire about the King's privy. It seemed that half of London had rushed down to the Thames to wave. People hadn't had a glimpse of their king for months. He'd hidden himself away in Whitehall, so seeing his privy was the next best thing.

'God save the King's privy!' yelled someone from the bank.

Superloo was having such a good time that it had to remind itself sternly of the purpose of its visit. 'This isn't all about YOU,' it lectured itself. 'You're here to rescue King Henry's close stool.'

On the other hand, they were going to Whitehall, weren't they? To the King's private rooms where Superloo had wanted to be all along. And, with any luck, its toilet relative would be there, waiting.

'So it's all good, as Finn would say,' Superloo crowed to itself. It thought briefly about Finn. Would he catch up? 'Of course he will,' the toilet answered its own question. 'A smart, resourceful boy like him!' An unfamiliar feeling fizzed through Superloo's circuits. Could it be doubt? It had to reassure itself again, quite firmly this time. 'He'll realize I'm going to Whitehall. I bet he's there already!'

Its worries settled, Superloo tuned in once more to the shouts from its adoring public.

Finn and Toby were on the river too. They were following Superloo to Whitehall. But they weren't powering along in the King's barge with flags flying and crowds cheering. They were beetling along, close to the bank, in a leaky old rowing boat. Toby had found it tied up to a wharf and borrowed it.

'Couldn't you have borrowed something better?' said Finn. Water slopped outside and inside the boat. As Toby rowed, Finn was bailing like mad with the cap that Mr Lew Brush had lent him.

*My ears are freezing*, thought Finn. And the back of his head felt strangely bare. For the first time since being in the stocks, he remembered his pudding-basin haircut. He put a hand cautiously up to his head. His hair felt very weird, like a wrap-around fringe. 'Wonder what it looks like?' he fretted. As soon as he found Superloo again, he was going to check it out in the cubicle mirror.

71

'Why did they cut off my hair?' he asked Toby.

'It be unlawful for apprentices to have long hair,' said Toby.

'Is *everything* against the law in Tudor times?' asked Finn. 'You can't move without getting arrested!' Suddenly, he realized something. 'Hey, I understood every word you just said,' he told Toby. He was finally getting used to Tudor English.

The river was busy with traffic, all kinds of boats. A big smelly sailing barge went past, crammed with *baaing* sheep. Rowing boats crowded at the landing stages. Boatmen looking for passengers bawled, 'Eastward ho! Westward ho!'

'Look out!' yelled Finn, bailing like mad, as big waves from some rich person's barge rocked their little boat and almost swamped it. They were passing magnificent mansions, with gardens right down to the river's edge. But Finn barely had time to glance at them. He was too busy bailing, too worried about not catching up with Superloo.

Toby gave a long, ragged sigh as he rowed. Roger, the sewer rat, came out and sat on his master's shoulder, nuzzling his cheek, as if to comfort him. For the first time, Finn really looked at the boy he'd met in the stocks. He remembered that, just like him, Toby had problems too.

'*Errrr*, I never said,' he told Toby, 'but thanks. Thanks for saving me from the stocks.'

Toby wasn't listening. He forced his poor weary body to row faster. 'I pray I am in time to save Sir Percival.'

Finn remembered too that, when they were in the stocks, Toby had told him about Sir Percival. How he'd been falsely accused of poisoning the King and taken to the Tower. How the King's doctor was the real villain. And how Sir Percival would get his head chopped off unless Toby found the proof to clear his name. Toby seemed to think a lot of this Sir Percival guy.

Finn asked, as he sloshed out more scummy water, 'This Sir Percival – is he your father?'

Despite his troubles, Toby gave a shout of laughter. Only a foreigner like Finn would ask such a stupid question. 'My father was a poor peasant,' he explained. 'Sir Percival is far above me. He is a noble knight. He is Groom of the Stool to King Henry.'

'Hey, I know about the Groom of the

73

Stool,' said Finn, pleased that at last he understood something about Tudor times. It would be a great opportunity to ask, 'Does he actually wipe the King's bottom?' It would answer a question of vital historical importance. Hadn't Superloo said boffins still argued about it? But Finn could see this wasn't the moment.

'I can never repay Sir Percival,' Toby was saying in heartfelt tones. 'Were it not for his kindness I would be a drain-raker still.'

'Oh, right,' nodded Finn, vaguely aware that Sir Percival had rescued Toby from something terrible.

But Toby knew the foreign boy didn't really understand. Nobody did who hadn't been a drain-raker. And only very small people or kids need apply because the drain tunnels were just one metre high. You worked underground, on hands and knees, in the sludgy, stinking dark, raking the muck out so the drains didn't clog. The foul air made you feel ill; sometimes you passed out. You had a candle but that only shed a feeble light. And in some drains you daren't use it. A single spark and that poisonous air could explode and the drain cave in and bury you. Two of Toby's friends had been lost that way. Toby gave a shudder, as if to shake off dreadful memories.

'Thanks to Sir Percival,' Toby told Finn, 'I was honoured with the post of Keeper of the Key of the King's Close Stool.'

'*Wow*, congratulations,' said Finn.

'Only I do not have the key,' explained Toby. 'Sir Percival took it.' He didn't know why he was fretting about that key when he had no job any more. And no hope of getting it back unless Sir Percival was freed. He turned to look over his shoulder. 'We are almost at Whitehall,' he said.

Finn saw a massive, majestic red-brick palace with tall windows overlooking the river. '*Wow*,' he said again. 'Is that where we're going?'

There was no sign of Superloo, just a few flower garlands floating on the Thames. The toilet genius was already inside. It had arrived at the King's own landing stage. Then it had been carried with great ceremony – a guard of honour and a trumpet fanfare – to Henry's private rooms.

But Toby didn't dare row any nearer for fear the porters, who patrolled the palace grounds, would recognize him. And besides, he had a question to ask Finn.

'I must go into Whitehall. For Sir Percival's sake. But must you? There will be great danger. And if we are caught . . .'

'I've got to go in there too,' said Finn firmly.

'For a privy?' asked Toby, shaking his head in disbelief. 'But what manner of privy is this that you should risk your life?'

Finn stopped bailing. '*Errrr*,' he began, his brain whirring. How could he explain Superloo to a Tudor boy? Where to start? A super-intelligent public convenience? That had brought him here from the twenty-first century? You couldn't make it up. Finn gave up. 'Look,' he said desperately, 'I can't explain. But I have to find that privy. I just *have* to.'

'Then we must seek Tib's help,' Toby told Finn, pulling into the bank. They abandoned their leaky boat and Finn scrambled after Toby up some slimy stone steps, straight into clouds of steam.

'Toby? Where are you?' cried Finn, blundering around.' Suddenly, he was through the clouds. He stared about. He seemed to have stumbled into an outdoor laundry. There were steaming washtubs standing on fires. And ladies down by the river, bashing clothes on rocks, spreading them out on bushes to dry.

Then he saw Toby next to a girl crouched over a washtub. She was up to her elbows in hot, greasy water, scrubbing away at something.

'This be Tib, my sweetheart,' said Toby, blushing. Tib stood up. There were no rubber gloves in Tudor times. Her hands were cracked and sore from the soap and lye. The hood of her cloak fell down to show ginger curls.

*It's her!* thought Finn. *The girl from the football game.*

They heard an angry bellow from down the street. 'You, Tib!' A large muscly lady came storming towards them.

'Oh no,' whispered Toby. 'It be Mrs Harris, the King's Washerwoman.' And Mrs Harris was on the warpath. She'd heard about Tib playing football with the boys. What a scandal! Especially when she should have been scrubbing clothes. This time, her unruly apprentice had gone too far.

'Tib!' screeched the fierce Mrs Harris. 'You rumpscuttle!' Mrs Harris fancied herself a fine lady ever since she became the King's personal laundress, the only one trusted to wash his undies. But when she was hopping mad, like now, some Tudor street slang crept in. 'Rumpscuttle!' she bawled at Tib again.

Superloo would have soon translated. '*Rumpscuttle*? That means tomboy, of course.'

Mrs Harris looked fit to burst. 'By my life!' she shrieked, her face crimson with rage. 'It was an ill day when I took you on as 'prentice!' She shoved Tib aside and, grunting with the effort, hauled something heavy and dripping from the washtub. She spread it out on the ground to inspect. It looked to Finn like a pair of knickers, but they were the biggest knickers he'd ever seen. Were they for an elephant?

Then Toby put him right. 'They be the King's slops!' he gasped in awe. 'That his Majesty wears next his skin!' He turned away, not sure whether he should be looking.

'*Slops?*' said Finn. But this time, he didn't need Superloo to translate. 'Are they *really* King Henry's underpants? Cool!'

But Mrs Harris was ranting on at Tib. Once again, her apprentice had disgraced herself. 'You idle wretch! There be a stain on the King's slops! That stain must come out afore these slops go back to Whitehall!' And she rampaged down to the riverbank to give her other workers an ear-bashing.

Miserably, Tib knelt down. She scooped

some black, jelly-like soap out of a pot, glooped it on to the King's pants, then started to scrub. But suddenly, she leapt up, her eyes flashing. 'I don't care a fig about the King's smelly old slops!' she cried.

'*Shhh*, Tib!' warned Toby, looking nervously round. Was anyone listening? It was probably treason to be rude about the King's underwear.

But Tib wouldn't be stopped. 'And I don't care about Mrs Harris!' she cried, a bit too loudly.

Mrs Harris had overheard. She bellowed from the bank, 'Begone then, you wretch! I'm well rid of you! You are my 'prentice no longer!'

Tib hated washing dirty clothes. She'd rather play football any time. But she'd just done a very rash thing. Unlike Toby, she wasn't an orphan, but her parents were too poor to feed her. She had to make her own way in the world. And how could she do that without a job?

'I must starve now,' she said woefully.

'Do not weep, Tib,' said Toby. 'When Sir Percival is free he will take care of both of us. But I am come to beg for your help.' And he began to explain to Tib, his voice low and urgent. Finn just couldn't catch the drift.

Then Toby finished by saying: 'So, good Tib, will you take my friend Finn into the palace? But only to the door of the King's private chambers. From there, he must seek the King's privy alone.'

'Wait a minute,' said Finn uneasily. 'Aren't you coming too?'

Toby looked grim, as if he was steeling himself for something. 'Aye, I am bound for the King's chambers, just as you are,' he told Finn. 'But I must go in through the drains.'

# CHAPTER TEN

**B**ack in the twenty-first century, the rogue robot hunter, Mr Hans Dryer, sat, unmoving. His hotel room was bleak and bare. He could see only a multi-storey car park from its windows. But Mr Dryer didn't mind that. The only thing that existed for him was his glowing computer screen. He'd baited the trap by putting the message from the lonely ladies' toilet out into cyberspace. Now all he had to do was wait.

Mr Hans Dryer's face was blank as always. Only his eyes showed a tiny gleam of excitement – the thrill of the chase. He believed in his job. He was doing the world a big favour. Every one of those metal freaks, those mutant machines, should be terminated.

He was sure the rebel loo would reply sooner or later. It wouldn't be able to help itself.

Mr Hans Dryer wasn't an expert in robot psychology for nothing. He could think himself inside their computer brains. He knew how they yearned for the company of others like themselves. How it was a longing that gnawed away at them constantly.

For an instant, Mr Dryer's eyes had a faraway look. Then they fixed themselves again on the computer screen. He wasn't impatient. His calm was icy. That's because he had no self-doubt: he was 100 per cent sure of success. He would get his robot – he always did.

Behind the Hi-Tech Toilets factory, in the Toilet Museum, Mr Lew Brush was pacing restlessly about, waiting for Superloo to come back.

'I'm worried, boy,' he confessed to his flatulent old hound. Blaster's sad, baggy face peered upwards. He knew his dear old master was troubled about something. And that made him anxious too. He gave a melancholy toot from his rear end.

Absent-mindedly, Mr Brush stroked his hound's moth-eaten fur. 'It's all right, boy, don't upset yourself. But I wish I knew what they were planning next.' Since the Special Forces had pulled out, no one seemed to be trying to terminate Superloo. But that made Mr Brush even jumpier. He knew the next attempt would be even sneakier. Much harder to detect than soldiers stomping round with guns.

'Keep busy!' Mr Brush ordered himself. He couldn't spend all day fretting. It might be teatime before Finn and Superloo reappeared. He set to work, clearing a space for King Henry's close stool beside Superloo's other famous toilet ancestors, King Tutankhamun's golden toilet and the Emperor Hadrian's latrine. There was getting to be quite a collection now.

Pity none of them had a brain between them. Finn and Mr Lew Brush had brains. But it was clear that Superloo often found its two human companions frustrating. It could be quite condescending. 'I pity you poor humans,' it would tell them pompously. 'I'd hate to have brains like yours. So slow and inefficient!'

'What that toilet really needs,' Mr Brush mused, 'is another super-intelligent loo to talk to.' But that wasn't going to happen. As far as Mr Brush knew, only one had ever been made. And that was by mistake. Superloo was unique.

Mr Brush went into his bedroom. It was a cosy little cubbyhole at the back of the museum. The Managing Director of Hi-Tech Toilets would have had a fit if he'd known that Mr Lew Brush slept at the museum. In fact, it was his only home, apart from a shed down at his allotment.

To make the time go faster, while he waited for the time-travelling toilet's return, he switched on his computer. Mr Lew Brush was a museum curator – but that didn't mean he was stuck in the past. He found modern tech-nology most useful for keeping up to date with toilet issues.

'Now, what's the latest hot news in the toilet world?' he wondered as he logged on to the website of the British Toilet Association. '*Hummm*, a toilet on wheels in Thailand that's pulled by a bloke on a bike. Fascinating! You can flag it down like a taxi!' That reminded him. After that wheels fiasco with Superloo, he'd promised to think of better ways to make the toilet mobile. He'd have to give that some thought.

He surfed the Net, hoping to find other

interesting toilet info. He clicked on an advert – for a modern toilet that could wash your bum and blow-dry it 'with wafts of warm, scented air'.

'*Huh!*' snorted Mr Brush, moving on. He wasn't interested in newfangled toilets. He preferred the old ones. 'The Victorian Age,' he murmured. 'Now that was the Golden Age of toilets.' The great Thomas Crapper, and Sir Walter Closet, who had owned the toilet factory, before it was taken over and ended up as Hi-Tech Toilets. His loo designs, the Clencher and the Maelstrom, were, in Mr Brush's eyes, toilet perfection.

*They were real craftsmen then*, thought Mr Brush. *None of this modern rubbish.* The only modern toilet he had any time for was Superloo. But who could resist a toilet with a brain?

Mr Brush was about to close his computer down when something caught his eye. 'What's this?' he said, peering at the screen. He put on his specs so he could see better. But he hadn't read it wrong.

'I am a super-intelligent, ladies-only public convenience . . .'

'Good heavens,' whispered Mr Brush,

gobsmacked. 'Look at this,' he told Blaster, who'd just come tottering in. 'That's incredible! And I thought Superloo was the only one.'

He thought, *I'll reply straightaway!* How thrilled Superloo would be if, when it returned, Mr Brush had already fixed up a date with this lonely ladies' loo.

*I can't wait to see its face*, he thought, forgetting for a second that Superloo wasn't human. But then he paused. *How do you address a ladies' loo?* He didn't want to be impolite. He was just going to type in 'Dear Madam' when he suddenly realized.

'You silly old fool,' he snapped at himself. If anyone was trying to get Superloo to reveal its whereabouts, this would be the perfect way, and much more sophisticated than sending soldiers with weapons.

'I bet it's a trap,' murmured Mr Brush. And he'd almost fallen into it. But should he reply anyway? Try to trap the trapper? That might be a risky move.

*This needs careful handling*, thought Mr Lew Brush. *I think I'll sleep on it for a bit.* He yawned. 'I'm just having forty winks, Blaster.' He had to tell the faithful hound he was only sleeping, otherwise, Blaster thought his dear old master was dead and got really, really upset. The last time that had happened, it had taken Mr Brush all day to clean up the Toilet Museum.

Mr Brush closed down his computer while he had a short siesta. When he woke up and his brain was fresh and sharp, he'd decide how to tackle this new challenge.

While Mr Brush and Blaster were snoozing in the museum, the Managing Director of Hi-Tech Toilets was staring out of his office window.

*Thank goodness all the fuss has died down,* he was thinking. He meant the fuss about the four-billion-dollar microchip, sent to his factory by mistake. It had really rattled him when those gun-toting soldiers had turned up. But now the soldiers had gone and no one else had arrived asking awkward questions. It seemed that Hi-Tech Toilets was in the clear.

*Back to business,* thought the MD. Now he could catch up on all those things he'd neglected. And the first thing he saw was a memo on his desk saying, 'Demolish Toilet Museum.'

'It's falling down anyway,' he told himself. He could see it from here – well, its roof at least, with its missing tiles and green moss. Everything about it was bad for the image of a modern, go-ahead company like Hi-Tech Toilets: the crumbling building, that ancient, cobwebby collection of loos inside and, most of all, that cantankerous old caretaker who seemed to be a law unto himself.

The MD was a bit scared of him though – of his strong, unflinching gaze. Mr Lew Brush seemed like a tough cookie. *If he finds out I'm going to knock his museum down, he'll go ballistic,* thought the MD.

What if Mr Lew Brush climbed on to the roof with a banner, 'SAVE THE TOILET MUSEUM'? Or stood in front of the bull-dozers yelling, 'I'm prepared to die for my toilets!'? What if his picture was in the local paper? Or, worse still, on the television news? The MD winced. That would be very bad publicity for Hi-Tech Toilets, who prided themselves on being a caring company whose motto was, 'Our Customers Are Number One!'

*No, that'll never do,* thought the MD. Then he had a brainwave. *I know. We'll demolish it at night after he's gone home. And when he turns up in the morning he can protest all he likes. It'll be too late to do anything. His precious museum will be rubble.*

He called out to his secretary: 'Doreen? Get me Dave's Speedy Demolition Services' email address, will you?'

'I want it done tonight,' the MD decided, 'before the stroppy old beggar gets wind of my plans.'

# CHAPTER ELEVEN

'There,' said Tib, with a mischievous grin, as she tied Finn's bonnet under his chin. 'What a pretty 'prentice wench!'

'Is this strictly necessary?' growled Finn, making his voice as deep and ungirly as possible.

'Aye, if you want to get past the guards,' said Toby.

'Why can't you dress as a girl too?' Finn asked him. 'And come in with us?'

Toby shook his head. 'The guards know my face too well. They would arrest me, even in disguise.'

Finn sighed, 'Suppose you're right. But I look a right prat.' He was wearing a long white smock, with a sort of sleeveless woollen frock over the top, and a white hood like a baby's bonnet. He tried to look on the bright side. At least the bonnet covered his pudding-basin haircut. And he didn't have to crawl through drains like Toby.

'Will I see you inside then?' Finn asked Toby. After all, they were both bound for the King's private rooms, he to find Superloo and Toby to get the evidence to clear Sir Percival.

'Perhaps,' said Toby. 'But if we do not meet again, Finn my friend, I hope you find your privy.'

'Yeah, thanks,' said Finn. But as they shook hands, Finn was squirming inside. He reminded himself, 'If it wasn't for this guy you'd still be in the stocks. You could at least offer to help.'

'Look,' he told Toby, 'maybe I can find my privy *and* help you get your evidence.'

'Truly?' said Toby. He looked grateful, like he'd be really glad of some back-up. 'Then wait for me at the door of the King's chambers. Where Tib leaves you.'

'I shall help find the evidence too,' declared Tib, tossing her head defiantly.

'No, Tib!' begged Toby. 'Show Finn to where I am waiting. But then leave the place entirely.' He couldn't bear to think of Tib being arrested, maybe charged with treason. 'Do you promise?'

'I promise,' said the headstrong Tib, with her fingers crossed behind her back.

Toby took Finn aside. He didn't want Tib to hear this. 'If I am not waiting,' he whispered to Finn, 'you must go on alone to Dr Slide's lodgings. You must find the evidence, take it to the King.'

'What, me?' said Finn, horrified. 'I've never met a king before. What do I do?'

'Kneel,' said Toby, repeating the rules of polite behaviour that Sir Percival had taught him. 'Be bare-headed, cast your eyes down, speak humbly.'

'Check,' said Finn, ticking the list off on his fingers.

'Also,' added Toby, 'in the King's presence, you must not yawn, puff out your cheeks or suck them in, whistle through your nose, lick your lips, furrow your brow, crook your neck. None of that is good manners. Nor must you –'

'I can't remember all that!' interrupted Finn, who'd run out of fingers. 'Look, I'm yawning now. And I didn't even know I was doing it!' He always yawned when he was scared; he didn't know why. 'What if I do something wrong? Like lick my lips? Look, I'm doing it already!' He got dry lips too, when he was afraid.

Toby frowned. Even Sir Percival had to walk on eggshells when he was waiting on the King. At any moment, Henry could lose his temper. 'He is like a madman,' Sir Percival had once confided. 'He sometimes foams at the mouth. And woe betide any who cross him.'

'Just do not displease the King,' Toby warned Finn. 'Especially, do not let forth foul stinks, pop your lice or scratch your codpiece.'

'My what?' said Finn.

But Toby wasn't listening. 'I must make haste,' he fretted. 'Time is wasting.'

Finn had thought of another problem. 'What about this evidence?' he called after Toby. 'I don't even know what I'm looking for!'

'Nor do I!' Toby called back. 'But we shall know it when we see it.'

'Oh, great,' muttered Finn as he disappeared. 'That's a lot of help, I don't think.'

'We must be gone too,' said Tib, 'before Mrs Harris comes back.' She was still down by the river giving her poor washerwomen a hard time. Tib thrust a basket into Finn's arms.

'It weighs a ton!' Finn complained. It contained six pairs of King Henry's enormous underpants, clean and neatly pressed, with lavender in between to make them smell nice.

Finn was still chuntering to himself: 'I can't remember all those rules!' He realized he was puffing his cheeks out because the basket was so heavy. 'Stop it!' he ordered himself. Surely Henry wouldn't chop your head off just because you puffed your cheeks? Was he really such a monster?

'This is crazy!' Finn decided. 'It's doing my head in!' Why had he ever offered to help Toby? Then he remembered yet another problem. *Oh, great!* he thought bleakly. As well as helping Toby, he still had to find that close stool. And hadn't Mr Lew Brush asked him for something? 'An antimony pill,' Finn reminded himself.

'What is an antimony pill exactly?' he asked Tib.

Tib looked at him with concern. 'Are your bowels troublesome?' she asked.

'Pardon?' said Finn. He thought he'd better not pursue that subject. Besides, they'd reached the gatehouse of the palace, where the Sergeant Porter stood on guard with other sentries, all armed to the teeth. A poleaxe came swishing down, blocking their path.

*Oh no*, thought Finn, his knees trembling. *I thought Tib said no one would stop us.* He hoped he didn't have to run in his long, flouncy skirt. But the guards only wanted a quick rummage through Henry's drawers, to make sure he and Tib weren't smuggling in any weapons. Finn kept his eyes down, like a lowly laundry wench should. Even Tib was keeping quiet, being very humble and obedient.

'Pass!' said the sentry at last, raising the poleaxe.

*Phew!* thought Finn. He was puffing his cheeks out, with relief this time. He sucked them in again. Oh no, that wasn't allowed either! 'Just forget all that good manners stuff for now,' he told himself. 'You only have to remember it if you meet the King.' And that was something he *didn't* plan to do if he could possibly help it.

Tib strode confidently ahead. She'd been this way many times with the King's laundry. No one gave her a second glance. But Finn was staring around: '*Wow!* This is flashy!'

Finn thought Tudor houses were gloomy places, all low ceilings and dark oak panelling. But Henry's palace was airy and spacious. It was gaudy with colours, like a fairground or

95

carnival! Bright tapestries and pictures hung everywhere. Silver plates and goblets, set with precious stones, glittered on chests and side-boards. Jewelled light streamed in through huge stained-glass windows. Even the wood panelling was painted blue and gold.

But who were this rowdy rabble, hanging about in the splendid rooms and galleries? After all Toby's talk about good manners, Finn had expected courtiers bowing to each other, being mega-polite. But this lot weren't polite at all. They were breaking every rule: spitting, scratching themselves, playing dice, getting drunk. Even popping their lice between fingernails.

'For heaven's sake!' Finn looked away. There was one peeing in a fireplace!

'They are servants,' explained Tib, 'with nothing to do.'

Since Henry had taken to his sickbed, things had gone to pot in the palace. Life was no fun for courtiers. There were no banquets or jousts any more. You couldn't get in to see the King because Dr Slide kept everyone out. Many nobles had got fed up and gone back to their country mansions. There was no one to order the servants about, so they were making the most of it.

A few nobles remained. A lady in a silk dress rustled by. Her clothes were fabulous, but her face was a shock. Her teeth were black stumps, but she flashed them proudly. Because sugar was so expensive in Tudor times, only the very rich could afford teeth that rotten. Her face was corpse white, caked with powder that cracked like crazy paving. And her lips were vampire red, as if she'd just been sucking blood from her latest victim.

'She looks like a ghoul!' Finn shivered. A courtier came waddling up the gallery to meet her. He was enormously big and wide, like a walking sofa . . .

'That's not HIM, is it?' asked Finn, almost dropping the basket. 'It's not King Henry?'

'Nay,' grinned Tib, shaking her head. 'He is just a lord.' There were usually loads of them at the palace, all hoping for a handout from the King. And the most grovelling ones had made themselves into Henry lookalikes. They had their beards and hair cropped short. They even had their clothes stuffed with horsehair to make them seem fat.

'He looks ridiculous!' scoffed Finn until he remembered he was wearing a dress. The two courtiers huddled in a seat in one of the great bay windows, whispering and plotting together.

'When the cat is away,' shrugged Tib, 'the mice will play.'

Finn was worried that the lord and lady might stop them. He pulled his white bonnet over his face and kept his eyes cast down. But he needn't have worried. The two nobles never noticed servants. Finn and Tib might have been invisible. Tib led Finn through the empty outer chamber to the big door carved with lions.

'The King is beyond that door,' she whispered. Even she sounded awed. She'd never been so close to the King's private rooms before.

'But where's Toby?' asked Finn. 'He said he'd meet me here.'

Tib looked worried. 'I will wait a little,' she said.

'But Toby said you shouldn't stay,' began Finn.

'I will wait,' declared Tib.

'*Oi!*' someone shouted. A porter appeared, carrying a poleaxe, one of the few still doing their duty, guarding the King. '*Oi*, you, wench! Stop where you be!' he yelled, striding towards Tib down the long gallery.

'Quick!' hissed Tib. 'Give me the King's slops!' She grabbed the basket from Finn and shoved him behind a tapestry that hung from ceiling to floor.

Finn heard the porter demand, 'What means this, wench? You have no business here. Do you mean harm to his Majesty? And were there not two of you?'

'Oh, good sir,' said Tib, bobbing a curtsey. 'Pardon me, it is just myself. And I mean no harm. I was lost.'

Behind the tapestry, flattened against the wall, Finn held his breath. Would the porter arrest Tib? Or just go away? Then, to his horror, he felt something tickling his face. Was it a spider? Every muscle in Finn's body tensed as it scurried over his nose. He felt a sneeze coming. He daren't put his hand up to brush the spider off. The porter might see the movement.

*Go away, spider, please*, begged Finn. But the spider stayed put. It seemed to think Finn's nose was a good place to spin a web. The tickling grew unbearable. The sneeze was swelling inside him. He just couldn't stop it! He gave a little choking splutter.

The quick-witted Tib heard and just before

Finn's sneeze exploded she dropped the heavy basket on the porter's foot.

The porter's scream of pain, '*OWWWWW!*', was much louder than Finn's '*Atishooo!*' He hopped around, holding his toes.

'Your pardon, sir, your pardon,' pleaded Tib, falling to her knees. 'It was an accident.' But it had put the porter in a really bad mood.

'You near broke my foot!' he roared. 'Begone, before I arrest thee! I will take the King's slops. Now begone!' To make sure she did, he watched her until she was out of sight.

Behind the tapestry, Finn heard Tib's feet pitter-pattering away down the long gallery. He heard the porter groan as he bent to lift the basket, and groan again as he limped away, carrying the King's undies.

Everything went quiet. Everyone seemed to have gone. Even the spider had scuttled off somewhere. Finn waited. He knew Tib couldn't come back, not while that porter was patrolling. But he was still hoping against hope that Toby might turn up. He kept peeking out, but finally had to admit it. 'He's not going to make it.'

Finn had no time to worry about what had happened to Toby. At this moment, he was more worried about himself, because now he had to go on alone. He'd promised Toby he'd get evidence from Dr Slide's lodgings, even though he had no idea where they were or what the evidence was.

'Superloo will know,' Finn assured himself. The super-intelligent toilet always did. All Finn had to do was find it.

He longed to be in the safety of that silver cubicle. To hear Superloo's quacky voice saying, '*Cha!* There's no need to panic. It's all easy-peasy! My super-intelligent brain has a plan!'

Finn took a deep breath. Once more he took a quick peek from behind the tapestry. There were no guards in sight. 'It's now or never,' he told himself. And he crept out from his hiding place. He opened the great heavy door, just a tiny bit. Then slipped through into King Henry's private rooms.

His heart was beating, fast as bongo drums. Did Finn think he might see the great ogre himself, propped up in bed? Well, he didn't. There were more rooms beyond the door, a maze of them, before you reached Henry's bedchamber. Finn's heart was hammering as he crept through. It felt like going deeper and deeper into a monster's den. His eyes were darting all over, expecting at any moment to hear Henry's roar or see the King's physician, the sinister Dr Slide, leap out from behind a tapestry and cry, 'Stop, you knave!'

'Not knave,' Finn corrected himself. 'You're a wench, remember.' But there was no sign of anyone. It was spookily silent in these secret rooms, after the chaos and noise in the rest of the palace. The only sound was the ticking of Henry's clock collection. Many rooms were in shadows. The shutters had been closed to keep out the daylight. They were stuffy too, as if no fresh air was allowed in.

Finn tiptoed on through this twilight world, seeing glints of treasure in the distance, rich colours here and there. Suddenly, a figure sprang out of the darkness.

'Aaaargh!' Finn leapt back. 'Your Majesty!' He dropped to his knees as Toby had told him and tried to remember all the other rules: no puffing out your cheeks, no letting forth stinks – good job Blaster wasn't with him. And no scratching your codpiece. Except he didn't have one of those, he was a wench. Were the rules different for girls?

'Your M-M-Majesty,' stammered Finn again, in what he hoped was a high, girly voice.

The King was towering above him, a fearsome, giant-sized figure. You couldn't mistake him. He glared down at the cowering Finn as if to say, 'Do you dare challenge ME?' He had his feet apart, hands on hips, and great puffy, jewel-covered sleeves. He looked like he had more ego than Superloo.

Finn knelt there, trembling, for a long, long time. But nothing happened. There was only silence, except for the steady ticking of the clocks. At last, he dared to glance upwards.

'You twit,' he told himself. What he'd seen was a life-size portrait of Henry, painted when the King was in the prime of life, in all his glory, in his most gorgeous clothes. The bloke in the picture looked so strong and healthy, he could wrestle a bear. Those were the days when Henry was best in the world at everything – at jousting, tennis, dancing, playing the lute. Although it would have been a brave courtier who told him any different or, in a jousting or tennis match, didn't let him win.

Finn got up off the floor. By now his nerves were in shreds. He called out softly, 'Superloo. Are you there?' Was there anyone alive at all, in this gloomy labyrinth?

He opened another door, just a tiny gap. A

great stink, like rotting flesh, hit him and someone shrieked like a child in a tantrum, 'Where is the key to my new close stool?' In a panic, Finn let the door shut. At the same time, from the shadows of the room he was standing in, came a familiar quacky voice.

'Finn? Is that you? It's ME. Superloo.'

# CHAPTER TWELVE

'**T**hey loved me, Finn,' Superloo was saying in a dreamy voice. 'I was a star! You should have seen the crowds. They were cheering, clapping. All for little ME. And someone shouted, "God save the King's privy!"'

But Finn had other things on his mind. He'd stripped off his laundry girl's disguise – he couldn't stand that clumsy skirt any longer, tangling round his ankles. But after he'd taken off his bonnet, he'd caught sight of himself in Superloo's mirror.

'This haircut,' raved Finn, 'is a complete disaster! It's a nightmare!' It was the worst haircut he'd ever had. And he'd had some stinkers in his time. You only had to look back at his old school photos. 'When I get back to the twenty-first century I'm going to have to go out with a bag on my head!'

Finn had loads to tell Superloo about what had happened since they'd split up in that alley. About Toby and Tib and Sir Percival, locked up in the Tower. But that would have to wait. Because, for the moment, that haircut drove everything else out of his mind.

'They put a basin on my head to do it!' complained Finn.

'Ah, the famous Tudor pudding-basin haircut,' said Superloo. 'They use the basin to get it level.'

'But it looks ridiculous!' Finn raved on. 'Everyone'll laugh. I look like a monk! I look like I'm wearing a really bad wig. I look like that kid in *The Simpsons*, what's his name? Ralph! I look like a total dork!'

'*Tsk, tsk, tsk,*' tutted Superloo. 'You humans! You do get upset over trifles.'

It was a good job the cubicle door was shut because Finn went red in the face and yelled, 'This is not a trifle! It's the worst haircut in the world! I'd probably look better with a trifle on my head than this!'

'*Shhh!*' said Superloo. 'Do keep your voice down. We're next to the King's bedchamber and his physician, Dr Septimus Slide, is in there with him.'

'How do you know that?' asked Finn, distracted from his hair for a minute.

'There isn't much I don't know,' said Superloo loftily. It was always keen to brag about the powers that made it far, far superior to humans. 'I heard them talking,' it told Finn, 'when the door was left open. But even before that I knew it was the King's bedchamber. My E-nose picked up the smell of his rotting bad leg.'

'*Phew!* Was that what I smelled just now? It was disgusting!'

But Superloo's E-nose just analysed smells; it didn't distinguish between nice and nasty. 'And,' continued Superloo, boasting some more, 'my E-nose also detected the ointment that's on it – made of raisins, garden worms, chicken fat, honeysuckle, powdered pearls, calf grease and red lead – the King's own recipe.'

'*Yuck!*' said Finn. 'Did that lot do any good?'

'Not the slightest,' said Superloo breezily. 'I expect it made it much worse. But what can you expect? The Tudors used mashed-up mole to cure baldness. They put a pigeon, chopped in half, on plague sores . . .'

But Finn was fretting about his hair again. 'I can't do a thing with it! It's hopeless!'

'For heaven's sake,' said Superloo. 'Just gel it when you get home.'

'I'd look like a pineapple then!'

'Then why don't you get your head shaved?'

Finn stopped shouting while he considered Superloo's suggestion. There was a kid in his class with a shaved head and he looked really tough. 'That's not a bad idea,' Finn admitted.

'A number two perhaps?' suggested Superloo.

'Even better,' said Finn. He knew his mum would never agree to a number one.

'OK, problem solved,' said Superloo. 'Now can we forget about haircuts? We're here to rescue my Tudor relative, remember? And we'd better get a shift on. My storage batteries won't last forever.'

'I was going to tell you,' said Finn. 'I met Toby. He's the Keeper of the Key of the King's Close Stool. I was in the stocks with him actually.'

'How convenient!' said Superloo, thrilled to bits. 'Where is this Toby? Introduce me! He'll know where my toilet ancestor is. That'll save us a lot of time searching. And, of course, I need the key to unlock it. That's absolutely vital.'

Finn said, in a troubled voice, 'Toby was supposed to meet me inside the palace, but he never showed up. I hope he's all right. But anyway, I promised to help him find the evidence to free Sir Percival.'

'Help *him*?' quacked Superloo, sounding distinctly jealous. 'But have you forgotten? You're here to help ME! What could be more important than rescuing my relative?'

'But this guy, Sir Percival, could lose his head!' Finn pointed out. 'Unless we find the proof that Dr Slide set him up.'

'Are you saying,' said Superloo huffily, 'that my toilet ancestor is worth less than a human being?'

Finn should have known: it was no use trying to reason with the offended toilet. When it came to its toilet relatives, it became more selfish and stubborn than ever. Finn decided he had to be sneaky.

'Anyway, even if Toby turns up, he hasn't got the key to your relative,' he told Superloo. 'Sir Percival has. And he's in the Tower. So you only get it if he gets out.'

'Well, why didn't you say so?' said Superloo. 'Then let's find the evidence to nail Dr Slide and free Sir Percival. And I think I know what it is!'

'You're a genius!' said Finn.

'I know,' said Superloo simply. It had only just finished telling Finn what the evidence was when it announced suddenly, 'There's someone moving about, here, in this chamber.'

'Dr Slide?' said Finn, his heart fluttering. 'King Henry?'

'Neither of those,' said Superloo, its sensors busy detecting, analysing the information. 'Not Dr Slide. And someone much, much lighter than Henry. From their footsteps, it seems they are sneaking. An intruder perhaps?'

'Toby,' whispered Finn. 'Open the door!'

Superloo didn't usually take orders. But this time it obliged, sliding open its cubicle door just a crack. It was as anxious as Finn to meet the Keeper of the King's Close Stool. 'I detect drains,' said Superloo instantly as its E-nose sniffed the air.

Finn peeped out into the shadows: 'It *is* him!' He wriggled out through the door and whispered, 'Hi, I'm here!' Toby's fine silk clothes were smelly rags. He was white-faced and shaking. 'You all right?' asked Finn.

Toby had blundered along pitch-black, stinking tunnels then scrambled up through a palace privy. That was enough of a shock – reliving those dreadful drain-cleaning days.

But something much worse had happened down there.

'R-Roger is lost,' Toby stuttered.

'Oh no,' said Finn. 'Your pet rat? That's really bad news.'

Toby nodded and gave a deep, hopeless sigh. Roger had smelled grey sewer rats, those that used to attack him. In a panic, he'd scuttled down Toby's leg and been lost in the dark. Toby had stayed down there longer than he should, shouting, 'Roger! Roger!' But he'd heard no answering squeaks. He'd seen no red eyes shining like rubies. He kept telling himself that Roger was a clever rat, that he'd find his own way out of the drains. If the grey rats didn't get him first.

'Want to hear some good news?' said Finn, anxious to cheer up his sad friend. 'It's about that evidence. Well, I know exactly what it is!'

'Truly?' said Toby. He stared at Finn, hope shining again in his eyes. 'Who told you this?'

'*Errr*, I overheard some people talking,' lied Finn 'Anyway, it's in Dr Slide's lodgings, like you said.'

'Dr Slide's lodgings may only be reached from the King's bedchamber,' Toby reminded him. Unless you climbed up to the palace roof, among the battlements and carved stone beasts, and went in that way. And Toby *definitely* didn't want to do that. He could manage drains, just about. But heights scared him stiff.

'The King's bedchamber is through there,' said Finn, jerking his thumb at the door. 'Let's go.' He wanted to get this over with as quickly as possible.

But Toby had a question to ask first. 'Is Tib safe? Did she leave the palace?'

'Yes,' nodded Finn. Toby looked so relieved that Finn couldn't tell him Tib only left because the porter made her. She'd planned to stay with them and share the danger. Finn had seen it in her eyes.

Toby strode purposefully to the door. Very gently, he opened it and took a peek. It seemed the coast was clear because he beckoned to Finn. They disappeared into Henry's bedchamber.

Behind them, Superloo said, 'Wait! I want to ask Toby about my toilet relative.' But its sensors told it that both boys had already left the room. 'Good luck, Finn,' whispered Superloo. 'Take care out there. I wish I was going with you.'

It was at times like this that it most longed

to be mobile. *Curse those supermarket trolley wheels*, it thought. It hoped Mr Lew Brush was thinking up something a bit more hi-tech.

It cheered itself up by playing its favourite tune, 'Drip, drip, drop little April showers', very softly to itself. At the same time, a low, dreary, droning sound came out of its speakers. That was Superloo, humming along.

Then it had another thought. Soon, when Finn found the evidence, Sir Percival would be freed. '*Wow!*' thrilled Superloo, all its chirpiness bouncing back. 'What an opportunity! I can talk to an actual Groom of the Stool!'

And settle once and for all that perplexing question: *Did he, or did he not, wipe the King's bum?*

# CHAPTER THIRTEEN

Finn and Toby crouched behind a massive suit of armour. It was one of Henry's, from his jousting days. It would have fitted a giant. A great mailed gauntlet hung down by Finn's ear.

Henry's bedchamber was vast, as big as a church, with a high, vaulted ceiling. It was crammed with stuff: furniture, clocks, suits of armour; maps, tapestries and paintings crowded the walls.

'*Phoarr*, it stinks in here,' whispered Finn. It was hot and stuffy too, from the fire blazing in a great marble fireplace, big enough to park a bus in.

'*Shhh!*' mouthed Toby while his eyes signalled, 'Look down there!'

Finn peeped out. He'd thought the room was empty, that Henry was somewhere else.

But he ought to have known from the smell –
there, in the shadowy distance, was a huge
carved bed piled with pillows and furs. A
massive mound rose from the middle of it, as
if a whale was tucked up under the covers.

*Henry!* thought Finn. That mound was all he
could see of the King. But flitting round the
bed was a bat-like figure in black robes, with
a long forked beard. It was the old Storm
Master himself.

'Dr Slide,' breathed Toby. Then '*Shhh*,' he
warned again. To get to Dr Slide's lodgings
they would have to pass quite close to Henry's
bed. If they got caught . . . But Toby didn't
dare think about that.

He tiptoed to take cover behind Henry's
tram. It was a kind of velvet-covered, portable
armchair. With his bad leg and enormous bulk
the King could barely walk, so servants had
to carry him from room to room. Toby waited,
his stomach churning, for Finn to make the
dash across from the suit of armour.

'*Phew!*' With a sigh of relief, Finn reached
the tram without being spotted. 'Where next?'
he hissed in Toby's ear.

Toby knew, vaguely, where the entrance to
Dr Slide's lodgings was. The servant lad, who

used to light Henry's fire every morning, had once described it. It was down at the far end of the room, under the portrait of Jane Seymour, one of Henry's six wives. Jane hadn't had her head chopped off – the portraits of those two queens were banned from the palace. But she'd died anyway, soon after giving birth to Prince Edward, Henry's son and heir.

Toby looked round, planning their route. And all the time, he was trying to keep one eye on Dr Slide. You never knew, with the wicked old wizard, where he would pop up next. But he never moved from the mound on the bed, fussing around it, plumping up the pillows.

Finn looked sideways. 'Tapestry?' he mouthed. He'd only been in Tudor times a few hours but he'd already found tapestries dead useful as hiding places. Didn't the Tudors realize their wall hangings were a big security risk? All over the kingdom, dodgy characters – thieves, assassins, evil plotters – were probably lurking behind them at this very moment.

And this one was vast. It showed St George slaying a ferocious, fire-breathing dragon. It hung from floor to ceiling, the full length of the wall.

Toby nodded enthusiastically. Why hadn't

he thought of the tapestry? He hardly even noticed them; they were like wallpaper to him. But, by using it as cover, they could reach the portrait of Queen Jane without being seen.

They slipped behind the tapestry and started sliding along, flattened against the wall. The tapestry was as thick and heavy as carpet so their bodies scarcely raised a bulge. It was suffocating behind there, hard to breathe. But, to Finn's relief, at least there were no spiders.

*Kerrunch!*

*What's that?* thought Finn, startled. His foot had crushed something. He looked down and dimly saw bent gold frames and broken glass.

Toby stopped dead too, his heart hammering. '*Gazers,*' he whispered. Finn had trodden on one of Henry's many pairs of spectacles. The King had loads of them; he left them all over the place. But had anybody heard the scrunch? Behind the tapestry, the two boys stayed absolutely still, their ears straining for sounds.

*We must be right opposite the bed!* thought Finn. They could hear Dr Slide's hissing voice, as he spoke to the sick King.

'Would Your Grace care for a licorice pastille? Or a soothing potion?'

'No, no!' came a peevish, imperious voice from the great walnut bed.

'Then now to that other great matter, most gracious Majesty,' Dr Slide grovelled. 'We have spoke of it before.'

Suddenly, the voice from the bed grew stronger, more savage. 'Hold your peace!' it roared. 'Trouble me no more! Those matters are settled! Cease to speak of it! Or I will see your head off before dinner!'

Dr Slide spoke again. But why wasn't his voice trembling? Why wasn't he begging for mercy? Instead, his voice had an edge of steel. 'Your Grace must bend to *my* wishes,' he began.

Behind the tapestry, Toby gasped. How dare Dr Slide speak to the King like that! Did he have a death wish? He expected Henry to yell for his Yeomen – there were still a few on guard – and have Dr Slide dragged away to the Tower.

But Dr Slide hadn't finished. 'Or, with my crystal ball, I will summon the thunder,' he threatened. 'Your Grace knows full well that they call me Storm Master.'

*So* that's *the power he has over the King*, thought Toby. He and Sir Percival had often wondered.

Everyone knew the King was as brave as a lion. The one thing that scared him was thunder – he crossed himself when it rumbled over the palace. That great hulking tyrant became like a scared little boy.

And his voice now was terrified, pleading. 'No, no,' he begged. 'I pray you, not the thunder!'

'Then will Your Majesty think on the matter?' asked Dr Slide in a voice still full of menace.

'I will bethink me,' came the voice from the great pillowed bed. 'I am minded to agree. But now let me sleep.'

Finn and Toby heard the crack of knuckles as Dr Slide rubbed his long, bony hands in glee. 'Most dread and gracious Lord,' he purred. He would say no more on the matter at present. Even he couldn't push the King too far. He could turn on you like a great wounded bear.

'Would it please His Majesty to try his new privy?' the boys heard Dr Slide hiss. 'It is in the outer chamber. They say it is all silver. Much more befitting Your Grace than this unworthy close stool.'

'Perhaps when I wake,' said the King, in a dozy voice.

*New privy?* thought Finn, horrified. *They mean Superloo!* Superloo would have a fit and Finn was scandalized too. The idea of anyone, even a king, actually using the great toilet genius *as a toilet* shocked him to the core.

But Toby was sliding on again. He'd reached the end of the tapestry and was peeking out. There was the portrait of good Queen Jane, hanging high above them. Toby scanned the wood-panelled wall beneath it.

*Where's the door to Dr Slide's lodgings?* he thought in a panic. Had that fool of a fire-lighter made a mistake? Taking a risk, he wriggled out of their hiding place to look closely at the wall. Finn stayed behind the tapestry, peeping out. Would Toby be spotted?

But Dr Slide wasn't looking in their direction. He was scrambling down from the monster bed piled high with furs and mattresses. He'd been up there all this time, clinging on like a poisonous spider, whispering into the King's ear. Now he held a flask of the King's pee aloft with his curled, horny nails. He swished it around before making a diagnosis. He didn't want the King to die too soon. At least not before he'd changed his will.

Behind him, the great lump in the bed snored and grunted. Finn still hadn't seen its face. But he did spy a large wooden box by the bed, its lid and sides studded with gold nails. It must be the close stool, Superloo's Tudor relative, still unused because Sir Percival had the key.

But Finn had no time to think about that. '*Pssst!*' said Toby, beckoning. He'd pressed the eye of a carved wooden eagle and, hey presto, a door had swung open. He should have known Dr Slide would have a secret entrance. Beyond it, twisty stone steps, just wide enough for one slim person, disappeared up into darkness.

Finn crept over from the tapestry, while the King snored and Dr Slide was still pee-gazing. Shutting the secret door softly behind them, he and Toby began to climb.

# CHAPTER FOURTEEN

'This place is really creepy,' shivered Finn.

He and Toby were standing in Dr Slide's lodgings. It was a tower room, crammed with all sorts of weird and spooky things – ingredients for magic potions and ghastly medicines. Little boxes were labelled in Dr Slide's spidery writing: monkey brains, unicorn horn, mermaid's tail. There was a human skull grinning from the table beside bubbling flasks.

*What kind of evil brew is that?* thought Finn. *Some kind of alchemy?*

There was another small door, which led out on to the palace roof. The only light came from window slits high in the tower, filled with thick green glass.

But Toby was asking, 'What is the evidence of which you spoke?'

'Oh, right,' said Finn, trying to remember everything Superloo had overheard. 'Dr Slide is trying to make the King change his will. He wants Henry to make him Lord Great Protector of Prince Edward.'

That didn't mean much to Finn, but Toby gasped. 'Sir Percival said Dr Slide was evil. But this is beyond all wickedness!' Prince Edward was only a child. When Henry died, he would need a Protector to help him rule. Nasty things often happened to princes with Protectors. Like the two poor princes in the Tower, they often ended up mysteriously dead. And their Protector became King in their place.

'If Dr Slide were made Protector,' said Toby, dismayed, 'Prince Edward would be killed and Dr Slide would rule England in his stead!'

'The evidence is the will,' said Finn. 'Dr Slide has forged a new will that names *him* as Lord Protector. And he's been trying to get the King to sign it.'

'And falsely accusing anyone, like Sir Percival, who might stop him,' said Toby. 'See this, Finn!' He held out a box full of green powder. He put a pinch into a water flask and shook it. It turned bright green and fizzy.

'This is how Dr Slide made it seem that the

King had been poisoned. I warrant I'll find blue power too. But, above all, we must find that will!'

They searched in the green, rippling light. They shook out dusty books of magic and medicine. Fat leeches, swollen with blood, squirmed in a dish. Finn looked under a jar that said *Lizards' gizzards*. His head was spinning a little. He felt unreal. Was it the fumes from Dr Slide's distillations? Or just the freakiness of his situation – here in this tower room, rummaging through a Tudor wizard's personal belongings? And this guy had some very weird stuff indeed.

'What's this?' Finn asked Toby. There was a crystal ball, as big as a human skull, on the table. Was it the one Dr Slide had spoken about, that he used to summon storms?

'Come on,' Finn mocked himself. 'You don't believe in that rubbish, do you?' But he couldn't help staring into its misty, swirling depths. He was about to pick it up so he could see better.

'Leave it be!' came Toby's scared voice. 'See, there be clouds in there.' Miniature black storm clouds hung in the little sphere. Finn leapt back. He'd seen a brilliant white flash between the captive clouds.

'Lightning,' came Toby's terrified voice. 'And do you hear that?'

'I don't hear anything,' said Finn. But he did hear it – a small but angry rumble of thunder from inside the crystal ball.

'Cover it up!' said Toby, shaking. He believed in witchcraft, magic and the power to summon storms.

'It's only some kind of trick,' said Finn. But all the same, he did what Toby asked. He threw a velvet cloth over the tiny tempest raging inside the crystal, for all the world as if Dr Slide had imprisoned it and could unleash it at his command.

They searched on. 'Methinks I have found it!' called Toby in triumph. He showed Finn a piece of fine white parchment – just the kind of page that could be slipped into the King's will, with no one the wiser. He turned it over, expecting writing naming Dr Slide as Lord Great Protector. But the other side was as blank as the first.

'Carry on searching,' sighed Finn. But how much time did they have before Dr Slide came back to his lodgings?

'Wait,' said Toby, who in his short time at Court had learned something about intrigue and plotting. A brazier burned in the corner, to keep the chill off the air. He held the piece of parchment above it, well clear, so it didn't scorch. 'See!' Words came up in the heat.

'It's magic!' cried Finn.

'No,' said Toby. 'This is no magic.'

'It's invisible ink,' said Finn, suddenly catching on. 'That's really sneaky.'

Toby nodded as more and more words appeared. People did this at Court if they wanted to keep their message private. They used milk to write with or onion juice, or even their own pee. 'What does it say?' he asked urgently.

Finn peered at the parchment, puzzling over the spidery writing. Then the words sprang at him off the page. He read them out loud. 'I do entrust the custody of my lawful heir, Prince Edward, to my loyal and loving physician Dr Septimus Slide and do hereby name him Lord Great Protector.'

'This is the evidence,' said Toby joyfully, 'which shall free Sir Percival!' He hugged the precious parchment to his chest. 'Now let us show this to the King,' he said, 'and he shall see who is the real traitor!'

'I think not,' said a soft, oozing voice behind them.

There stood Dr Slide, holding the flask of the King's pee. As well as his main ambition of becoming King, he had a nice little sideline in making medicine from royal wee. People paid a fortune for it. They thought it was a miracle cure for anything from piles to plague.

Dr Slide put the flask down carefully. He didn't seem at all alarmed. He recognized Toby, of course. He didn't know who Finn was, but he didn't care. Two scruffy, dung-spattered urchins were no challenge. Not when he had the King of England under his thumb.

But he must get rid of them for good. They'd seen too much. The will, for a start, and the powders he'd added, secretly, to the King's pee to make it seem as if Sir Percival had poisoned him.

'I fear,' he hissed at them, blocking the door to the stairs so they couldn't escape, 'that you cannot be allowed to live.' He seemed quite casual, even cheery about it. He stroked his forked beard with a curled nail and bared his yellow ratty teeth in a grin. Then he got serious. He turned the full power of his hypnotic gaze on Finn.

'Do not look into his eyes!' warned Toby. But it was too late.

If he'd felt dizzy before, now Finn's brain was a foggy blur. He stared deep into those glittering, cobra eyes. Soon he didn't know where he was, even who he was. He was just a slave to that stare.

'Stay there,' Dr Slide commanded him. 'And do not stir.'

Zombie-like, Finn obeyed. Toby stared frantically into his friend's face. But there was nothing there – it was as if Dr Slide had temporarily switched off Finn's brain. Now there was only Toby to deal with. Toby tried to dodge by Dr Slide and run down the stairs to the King's bedchamber, but Dr Slide was ready for that.

He whipped out a sword that he kept hidden under his robes. He began to swish the air. Toby leapt away. Dr Slide was scarily nimble. When younger, he'd been a master swordsman and he still hadn't lost his skill.

'Back, back,' he snarled, as if to a disobedient dog, forcing Toby towards the door that led out on to the palace rooftops. Toby didn't want to go. He clutched the will tightly.

'Put it down upon the table,' hissed Dr Slide. Grimly, Toby shook his head. It was all he had to save Sir Percival from execution. All the time, he tried to keep his face turned, to avoid the full force of that magnetic, mind-scrambling stare.

'*Put – it – down,*' ordered Dr Slide in his chilling whisper. He darted forward. With a swish of his sword, he ripped Toby's doublet sleeve. He didn't want to draw blood and make the will all messy. Besides, he wanted to make Toby's death seem like an accident, not murder.

'Put the will down,' he repeated, darting forward again and holding the sword at Toby's throat, 'or I will skewer you!' Toby dropped the parchment on to the table.

'Good knave,' said Dr Slide, forcing Toby back with his sword point towards the roof door. 'Now out on to the roof.' Dr Slide left the will on the table but as Toby backed through the door, the wizard scooped up his crystal ball.

Toby crouched among the statues of mythical beasts – the stone griffins, dragons and unicorns. He was shivering now, trying to fight off panic. He hated heights: just the thought of them made him feel sick and dizzy.

'Don't look down!' he told himself. The Thames was a wide silver ribbon far below, the ships like toy sailing boats. But what was happening to the sky? It had been blue before, but now a great wind gusted across the roof. Black clouds came rushing from all directions, hiding the sun. The day went suddenly dark as night.

Dr Slide didn't need his sword now. He threw it aside, and from the shelter of the tower room door, the Storm Master began stroking the crystal sphere, chanting spells.

'Thunder, lightning! You are free!
Take to the skies thunder, roar like a lion!
Lightning, sizzle and burn him!'

From the clouds overhead came an ominous rumble. Toby was hanging on to a unicorn's neck. He looked up, terrified. There was a sudden blue flash. A jagged lightning fork hit the roof and shattered a stone lion beside him into smoking ruins.

*Missed*, thought Dr Slide. But no matter, Toby wouldn't escape the next bolt. Dr Slide laughed wildly. He put his crystal ball down on the roof and swept his arms about as if conducting an orchestra.

'Rage, rage!' he screamed into the teeth of the storm as his black cloak whipped about him. This storm was his biggest, his best production yet. And it would serve a double purpose – incinerate Toby and scare the King into finally signing that piece of parchment.

Toby scuttled away like a crab as the storm grew wilder. He cowered under the battlements, covering his head, while the tempest raged. In the open door, Dr Slide's black robes billowed. Above them, thunder boomed and lightning crackled, getting ready for the next strike.

'Awake! Awake!' yelled a voice in Finn's ear. Someone was roughly shaking him. He seemed to be climbing back up out of a deep dark hole.

'Finn!' screamed the voice again. Suddenly, Finn's mind snapped back. 'Where am I?' he gasped, bewildered. 'Who are you?'

A boy was shaking him, a servant lad in the King's scarlet livery. The boy pulled his cap off, releasing a tangle of ginger curls. ''Tis me!' said Tib, shouting above the storm. She was dressed as the boy who lights the King's fires. He'd carelessly left his clothes in a heap while he splashed in the King's marble fountain, so Tib had borrowed them, to disguise herself.

'Tib!' Everything came rushing back. Finn's brain was filled with whirling thoughts. He didn't know what to say or do first. 'The will,' he gabbled, pointing at the parchment on the table. 'Dr Slide forged the King's will.'

'Where is Toby?' Tib was asking. But, at that moment, from the corner of his eye, Dr Slide spotted them.

'That rascal laundry wench!' he snarled, looking round for his sword.

'Go!' Tib yelled at Finn. 'Take the will! Show the King!'

Finn was torn by indecision. Should he go? Leave Tib and Toby to Dr Slide? Thunder crashed over his head; he couldn't think straight. Still he hesitated.

'Go!' shrieked Tib as Dr Slide leapt into the room. 'You are our last hope!'

Finn grabbed the will and dashed for the stairs.

Tib saw Toby, huddled outside while the storm howled about him like a wolf pack. Using her footballing skills, she dodged Dr Slide's flickering blade. As she raced through the open door to reach Toby, Dr Slide made the mistake of running after her. One deadly thrust would finish her off. Then he would

pursue Finn, yelling 'Assassin!', run him
through and retrieve the will.

Right above him a cloud glowed an evil
yellow. He heard crackling. Two last thoughts
flashed through his head. One was, 'Fool!' He
should have left Tib to the lightning. And the
other was, 'You can't kill me. I am Storm
Master!'

A fiery bolt came sizzling down. *Sssssss!*
There was a sound like frying fish. Dr Slide
keeled over, stiff as a kipper, his beard smoking,
struck by the very same lightning he'd just
released from his crystal ball.

Finn crept down the twisty stairs. He tried to
forget what was happening in the tower and
concentrate on what he had to do. Somehow,
he must convince the King. His mind was
swarming with all the rules of polite behaviour – kneel, speak humbly, keep your eyes cast
down, don't suck your cheeks in, don't puff
them out. He was bound to get something
wrong!

The bedchamber had changed. It wasn't
quiet with clocks ticking. Now it seemed alive.
Thunder rattled round the room. Great silver
flashes lit up tapestries, suits of armour, crossed

axes on walls. With all the crashing, banging and lightning bolts, it seemed like the end of the world had come. A great hulk in a nightgown thought so too. It was kneeling by the bed. Its legs were wrapped in stinking bandages. It had a linen nightcap on its head.

*The King!* thought Finn, dropping to his knees too. He was dumbstruck, overcome with awe and fear. He was just an ordinary twenty-first-century kid, face to face with King Henry VIII. His pong was terrible. But it certainly wouldn't be polite to say, '*Phew!*' or even wrinkle your nose.

Henry turned his massive head towards Finn. He had piggy eyes and wobbly jowls, and a tiny, pursed-up, cat's-bum mouth. 'Save me!' the cruel tyrant moaned, crossing himself frantically. 'Save me!'

Up on the roof, Toby and Tib stared at the doctor's stretched-out figure. It didn't move.

'Be he *dead*?' asked Tib.

'Take care,' said Toby as Tib approached. The doctor was a wily old fox; he could be pretending. Tib poked the body with her foot. The eyes stayed closed; not a curly nail twitched.

'He be dead as a doornail,' pronounced Tib, with a satisfied nod.

The storm was easing up. The thunder had stopped and the black clouds were scudding away. Suddenly, the sun broke through, warming up the cold stone of the dragons and unicorns.

'We must help Finn,' said Toby, forcing his wobbly legs to move, trying not to look down at the dizzy drop over the battlements. He staggered across the roof, towards the tower.

'Wait,' said Tib. She was peering into the crystal ball that Dr Slide had put down. A tiny scaled-down version of the storm they'd just seen raged inside it – perfect little storm clouds, tiny jagged lightning forks.

''Tis wicked magic!' declared Tib. And she booted the crystal sphere, as if it was a football, over the battlements. It curved through the air and smashed into a thousand glittering pieces in the courtyard below. 'Now no evil sorcerer can conjure up storms,' she said.

'Dear Tib,' said Toby, shaking his head, 'you should not have come back. But I am most heartily thankful you did!' Together, they went down to Henry's bedchamber.

As they passed Dr Slide's table, Toby slipped

some powder into the leather pouch at his belt – just in case the King wanted a demonstration of how his pee had been turned green and fizzy.

Something gleaming caught Tib's eye. 'Finn has need of that,' she said.

'Truly?' said Toby, grimacing. Personally, wild horses wouldn't make him swallow an antimony pill. But before he dashed after Tib down the stairs, he slipped it into his pouch too.

# CHAPTER FIFTEEN

Tib and Toby heard Henry shrieking. 'Bring Dr Slide! He will stop the thunder. Bring him here to me or I will have your head! I will have everyone's heads on spikes!'

They crept into the bedchamber. Where was Finn? He was nowhere to be seen. Henry was ranting to empty air. Even in a nightgown, supporting his huge bloated body on a walking stick, the King was a fearsome figure.

Toby's throat was dry, his heart pounding, but he walked straight up to the King. He fell to his knees, bowed his head and said, 'Most dread and honoured Majesty, Dr Slide is dead.' There was silence. How was Henry taking the news? Quaking, Toby dared to raise his eyes.

'Do you mock me?' the King snapped, staring down at him, his piggy eyes glittering fiercely in his great puffy face, his cheeks purple with rage.

'No, Sire, no. I have seen it with my own eyes.'

'It is really so?' whispered the tyrant to himself.

'Sire,' added Tib, with a deep curtsey, 'I have seen it too. He was struck down by his very own lightning. And see, his thunder has ceased.' She threw open a shutter. Winter sunlight came flooding into the bedchamber.

And suddenly, Henry laughed. He threw back his great bull-like head and roared with laughter. 'Then I am well rid of him!' he cried. 'I always hated that creeping toad.' Henry had feared him too, been under his spell. But he would never, ever have admitted it.

'Sir Percival called him that, a creeping toad,' said Toby timidly.

'Did he so?' roared the King, who seemed suddenly in a good humour. 'Then he is a wise man!' He seemed to have forgotten that he'd sent Sir Percival to the Tower under sentence of death. Now was the perfect time to remind him and to show him the will.

'Finn!' called Toby urgently 'Finn!'

Finn came hurrying out from behind a

138

tapestry where he'd hidden to escape Henry's tantrum. He handed Toby the parchment and backed away again. Best to leave the explanations to Toby and Tib. But, like Henry, he could hardly believe what he'd just heard – that Dr Slide was gone. He could still see the doctor's hypnotic, laser-beam eyes. Eyes that seemed to burn into your brain. Finn shook himself. 'Get a grip! He's dead, right?' he told himself. 'He's not coming back.'

Toby and Tib didn't have to talk for long. Henry clipped his spectacles to his nose and scrutinized the forged will. 'I *knew* that man was a villain. Now I see he was a traitor too! Why did no one tell me before? And did I not say Sir Percival was an innocent man?'

Of course, nobody said, 'No, you didn't.' All three nodded their heads in agreement. You never, ever disagreed with the King. Even if you'd brought him good news, he could turn on you in an instant. But, for the moment, he seemed really jolly. The Court had been waiting for him to die, but he wasn't quite ready to do that yet. Dr Slide's death had given him a new lease of life.

'I have been abed too long!' he shouted.

'Bring me orange pie and stewed sparrows. Where are my servants, my gentlemen of the bedchamber?' Then, as Finn watched from the shadows, everything went manic.

'The old wizard is dead!' The word spread like wildfire through the palace. 'And the King is up and about!' Servants put on their livery, hurried back to their posts. The cooks began stoking up fires in the kitchens. Grovelling courtiers kept out by Dr Slide came crowding back in, bowing and scraping. Henry seemed back to his old self, shouting orders and bullying everyone.

'Send for the Queen! Fetch my Lord Chancellor!' Messengers were clattering through the courtyards, riding off from the palace in all directions.

'Where are my Yeomen of the Guard?' screamed Henry. His bodyguard came crashing in, armed to the teeth. 'Why did you arrest Sir Percival,' demanded the King, 'and convey him to the Tower?'

No one dared say, 'Because you told us to.' Henry always had to have someone to blame for his wrong decisions.

'Go and release him,' ordered the King. 'And take my true and loving servants with you!' He indicated Tib, Toby and Finn. Tib and Toby hugged each other for joy. Sir Percival's life was saved!

Finn was pleased too. But he'd never met Sir Percival. And he felt left out of everything, all this bustling, all this rushing about. *Time to go home*, he thought. He'd done what he promised, helped find the evidence to free Sir Percival.

Then he heard something that decided him absolutely. 'Summon my tram!' Henry was shouting. 'Convey me to my new silver privy. I am minded to lay siege to it. I have not moved my bowels for near on a week!'

*Ugggh!* thought Finn, shuddering at the thought. He must rush to warn Superloo. But first, he had to make his excuses to Tib and Toby.

'I'm not coming with you,' he told them. 'I've got things to do.' They looked surprised.

'Farewell then, Finn,' said Tib.

'You were our true friend,' said Toby. They shook hands. But then the Yeomen started marching out and Finn could see Tib and Toby were itching to follow. They wanted to free Sir Percival from the Tower before Henry changed his mind.

Then Toby suddenly remembered something. 'I have a gift,' he said, rummaging in the leather pouch at his belt. He gave Finn what looked like a silver bullet.

'What is it?' said Finn.

'An antimony pill,' said Tib. 'Did you not say you had need of one?'

'Oh, right,' said Finn. 'I forgot about that. Thanks! Thanks a lot!' Mr Lew Brush would be thrilled.

He watched them hurry after the guards and out of his life. He stood for a moment, unnoticed, taking one last look at the Tudor scene – Henry's servants struggling to load him in his mobile armchair, while he shrieked curses when they jogged his bad leg.

'What are you standing here for?' Finn scolded himself. 'Get moving!' He dashed for the bedchamber door but then skidded to a stop. The close stool – Superloo's ancestor! There it was, locked up, forgotten, pushed into a corner. It wasn't that big – about the size of Finn's bedside cabinet at home. But when he tried to shift the wooden box, dragging it along by its leather strap, it was heavier than he thought. He'd need help. But there was no time. Henry, impatient to visit his new silver privy, was shouting for his servants to hurry.

Finn went rushing through to Superloo, slipping in through the crack in the cubicle door. 'It's me! I'm back!'

'Did you get my toilet relative? And what about the key?' quacked Superloo.

*Typical!* thought Finn. *It hasn't even asked about Sir Percival.* But he had to say, 'No, sorry. I need help to shift the close stool. And Sir Percival's still got the key. They've gone to release him. We can wait if you like, but King Henry's on his way. He wants to use his new privy.'

'What!' squawked Superloo. 'You mean he wants to use ME as a toilet? He thinks that's all I am?' Its voice was quivering with indignation. In its previous time-travelling trips, it had been worshipped as a god. It had been consulted for its wisdom. It had been treated like a celebrity. But it had never, *ever* been used as a mere toilet.

'It's disgraceful!' huffed Superloo. 'I thought perhaps Henry and I could discuss politics, philosophy, and all he wants to do is *poo* in me!'

'And he hasn't been for a week,' Finn pointed out in dark, sinister tones. 'I heard him say so.'

'Right, that's it!' said Superloo. 'We're out of here!'

'What, even without the close stool?' said Finn.

He'd expected the toilet to make more fuss, to rage, 'No way am I leaving without my relative!' But it was already flashing its cubicle lights and shrieking, 'Blast off!'

Finn clung on to the toilet bowl grimly as the cubicle started to spin. Soon the world became a silver blur.

Up on the palace roof, the sun was setting. Blood-red streaks slashed the sky, bathing the stone dragons in crimson light. It seemed as if they were breathing fire.

Dr Slide's body still lay untouched. No one had got around, yet, to dragging it away. Suddenly, a curly nail twitched. An eyelid shot open, shut again, opened again to show a beady snake eye.

*I'm alive!* thought Dr Slide, amazed. The lightning bolt had only stunned him. He sprang to his feet and dived into his lodgings. *Curses!* The will was gone. He wondered what mischief those three rascals were making. Perhaps it wasn't too late to stop them. He headed for the stairs. But at the top, he heard Henry roaring from his bedchamber.

Henry was in a really bad mood again, especially now his silver privy was mysteriously missing and his new close stool was still locked. Servants were racing about, on pain of beheading, to find a replacement. 'Else I shall burst!' shrieked the King.

'Fetch me that traitor Dr Slide's body!' he bellowed. 'Even though he is dead, I want his head on a spike!'

*Oh dear*, thought Dr Slide. *What ill luck!* He could see it was too late to sort things out – even for someone of his talents. And he'd been so close. 'The great monster was minded to sign that will this very afternoon,' he sighed to himself.

But no matter. He refused to be downhearted. There were guards coming up the stairs. He rushed back through his lodgings and, like a great bat with black flapping wings, he began leaping away across the roofs of Whitehall, springing over stone beasts and battlements, until he vanished into the night.

# CHAPTER SIXTEEN

Superloo made a perfect landing in the Toilet Museum. Finn stumbled out, dizzy as usual from the trip. Where were Mr Lew Brush and Blaster? He found them dozing in Mr Lew Brush's bedroom. The decrepit old dog was twitching and whining in his sleep. Was he dreaming of chasing rabbits, as he'd done in his younger days?

Finn tiptoed back to Superloo. 'I didn't wake them,' he told the toilet. Old codgers like Mr Lew Brush needed their rest.

Finn took off his smelly, coal-sack clothes and dumped them in the bin outside. It was always hard, this coming back. He was thinking of twenty-first-century things like texting his mates, having a pizza for tea. But part of him was still back in Tudor times.

'You don't think that guy, Dr Septimus Slide,

really was a wizard, do you?' he asked Superloo.

'A wizard?' scoffed Superloo. 'No way! You humans might believe such superstitious twaddle, but I have a logical computer brain. The man was a quack, a con artist. There were loads of them around in Tudor times, still are in fact. And that storm was just a coincidence.'

'But it came out of nowhere. It was a sunny day before!'

'British weather,' quacked Superloo. 'It can change in the time it takes to flush my toilet bowl.'

'But that doesn't explain the crystal ball,' protested Finn.

*'Cha!'* said the toilet scornfully. 'Just some kind of magic trick.'

'Suppose you're right,' said Finn.

'Of course I am,' said Superloo.

'I'm surprised you're not more upset about your Tudor relative,' said Finn. 'You know, having to leave it behind.'

Superloo gave a choking sob. 'Well, I am trying to be brave,' it sniffed. 'But to tell the truth,' it quacked, its voice suddenly chirpy again, 'I'm not all that fussed. I've found out there's a *much more* famous close stool here in the twenty-first century. It's on show to the public at Hampton Court. It was sat on by the royal bum of Elizabeth the First!'

'No,' said Finn. 'I am *not* nicking your close stool relative from Hampton Court. So don't even bother asking.'

'But I have a plan. It's foolproof! And it doesn't even involve time travel. First, we take the train to London –'

'No, no, no,' said Finn. 'I don't want to hear it!' He'd had quite enough of Superloo's rescue missions. His mobile rang. 'Oh no. It's Mum.' She'd be having kittens. He hadn't checked in since this morning.

'Yeah, Mum, yeah, yeah, yeah,' he gabbled into his phone. 'Sorry, sorry, sorry. Yeah, I'm on my way. Yeah, right this minute.' All his thoughts now were turned towards home and how he was going to persuade Mum to let him shave his head. And another thing: 'Have you got a woolly hat?' he asked Superloo. He didn't want any of his mates to see him with a pudding-basin haircut.

'Oh, never mind,' said Finn. 'I'll just put my hood up. Right, I'll see you tomorrow morning after I've played football.'

Five seconds after Finn had gone, Superloo

sighed, 'I'm bored.' It was a great toilet genius but, like a little kid, it loved being the centre of attention. It flushed its bowl loudly a few times to try and wake up Mr Brush. But all it heard from the bedroom was his gentle snore and a sort of wheezing, gurgling sound from Blaster, as if the ancient hound was being strangled in his sleep.

To amuse itself, Superloo began to surf the Net, looking for the next toilet relative to rescue. Then, '*Wow!*' it shrieked suddenly. 'I can't believe it!'

This time Mr Lew Brush heard. He came staggering out of his bedroom, his hair up in spikes, his eyes bleary. 'You're back! I slept longer than I meant to. Where's Finn?'

'Oh, he's gone home for his tea. But listen to this!' said Superloo in huge excitement. '"I am a super-intelligent, ladies-only public convenience. With no-touch flushing and auto-matic self-cleaning . . ." I'm in love already!' warbled Superloo.

'I've seen it,' said Mr Brush. 'It's on a website called *Lonely Loos*.'

But Superloo wasn't listening. It was rushing to tell him the rest. '"Are YOU a lonely toilet genius? If you are, I'm dying to meet you!"'

'Look,' said Mr Lew Brush, frowning. 'If I were you, I'd think twice about replying. Things on the Net aren't always what they seem. People pretend to be what they're not.'

'I know that!' burbled Superloo. 'But this is no scam. I can tell it's from another toilet. We're so alike! She could be reading my mind!'

'It could be a trap,' warned Mr Brush. He was no psychologist, but he realized Superloo only thought this was genuine because it wanted it so badly to be. 'Don't reply,' he cautioned Superloo again, 'at least until we've looked into it a bit more.'

'Are you kidding?' yakked Superloo. 'I've replied already. I want to grab this babe before anybody else does!'

'Are you, *errr*, a *male* toilet then?' enquired Mr Brush delicately. He'd never thought of Superloo as either male or female.

'Oh, I don't know!' quacked Superloo impatiently. 'When you're in love, do little details like that matter? Want to hear what else I said? I told her all about myself. I told her I'm a pop-up loo – that should impress her. I told her about my mighty brain and how sensitive and caring I am, with a great sense of humour . . .'

'You didn't,' interrupted Mr Brush urgently, 'tell her where you *lived*, by any chance?'

'Of course I did!' raved Superloo. 'She might have wheels that work better than my ones did. She might want to come rushing round here to see me.'

'You should never,' said Mr Brush sternly, '*ever* reveal any personal details on the Net.' He couldn't believe the great toilet genius had done something so stupid. It *knew* people wanted to hunt it down and terminate it. But love had obviously scrambled its circuits. It was behaving like a love-sick teenager: it had gone totally loopy!

'I wonder what she looks like?' it was raving. 'Do you think she's got a jumbo bog-roll dispenser?' But alarm bells were ringing very loudly in Mr Brush's head.

He hurried to the Toilet Museum door and opened it to check outside. It was dark by now. The workers had all left the Hi-Tech Toilets factory and gone home. It was very quiet out there. Mr Brush saw nothing suspicious. All he heard was an owl hooting in the distance. Nevertheless, he locked the doors and turned off all the lights, so anyone turning up would think the place was empty.

But that didn't calm his fears. He paced about nervously in the moonlight that washed over his precious toilet collection. 'I've got a very bad feeling about all this, boy,' he told Blaster. 'I just wish Superloo hadn't sent that reply.'

'*Gotcha*,' murmured Mr Hans Dryer in his hotel room.

The only sign that he felt triumphant was that his eyes glittered briefly. But his job wasn't finished yet. He'd located the rogue toilet. Now he had to terminate it and retrieve that microchip. His icy-cold professionalism cracked just a little as his lips curled into a chilling smile. He always looked forward to the termination bit. Robots could never be human, no matter how much they tried to be. They were nothing but metal freaks who didn't deserve to live.

He emailed his bosses to tell them he was closing in for the kill. Then he called for a taxi.

'Toilet Museum, guv?' said the driver when Mr Dryer climbed in. 'You'll have to give me directions. I didn't even know there *was* a Toilet Museum.'

\*

There wouldn't be for much longer. Superloo regularly hacked into the Hi-Tech Toilets emails – just to see what the Managing Director was up to and maybe pick up some tips about who was on its trail. But love had driven every other thought out of its brain. Otherwise, it might have read the reply to the MD from Dave's Speedy Demolition Services: 'No problem! By tomorrow morning, your Toilet Museum will be history!'

# CHAPTER SEVENTEEN

**N**ext morning it was too foggy to play football so Finn went early to the Toilet Museum. As he trudged along, his mind was full of his own personal problems. His haircut was top of the list. He'd borrowed his big brother's head shaver. He'd watched the DVD that came with it, called 'How To Use Your Head Shaver'. But it was harder then it looked. His hair, what was left of it, now looked like a badly mown lawn. That's why he was wearing his black woolly hat, pulled down to brow level. Mum had gone ballistic: 'Just *what* did you think you were doing?'

Gran had stood up for him, like she always did. 'Awwww,' she'd said, running her hand over his head. 'Don't tell him off. He looks like a cute fuzzy duckling.'

Finn scowled at the memory. He swung into

the Hi-Tech Toilets car park. The fog muffled noises, like walking through clouds. But it was quiet too because it was Sunday. There were no workers about; the whole place was shut down.

'How long does hair take to grow?' Finn was fretting. 'I know, I'll gel it!' Spiky was cool. Cute fuzzy duckling definitely wasn't. He walked out of a dense patch of fog.

'*Whaaaa?*' He stopped in his tracks. At first he couldn't believe what he was seeing. He actually rubbed his eyes, looked again. They'd been right first time. The Toilet Museum wasn't there. It was just a great big rubble mountain.

It was a terrible shock. Finn forgot to breathe. He just stood there, gawping. Then he sucked in a great gulp of air. His mouth still couldn't make proper words: '*Whaaa? Whaaa?*' But his brain sparked into life. Ghastly thoughts sprang up like monsters. What about Mr Brush, Superloo, Blaster?

Distraught, he leapt on the rubble pile and started tearing it away with his bare hands. Then, out of the mist, came a voice quite near – a stranger's voice. Finn stopped and crouched, very quiet.

'It all went smoothly,' said Dave of Dave's Speedy Demolition Services. 'The old guy had gone home like you said. The place was in darkness, all locked up. So we just rolled the machines in and smashed it down. Didn't take long.'

'That's because it was half falling down already,' said the MD of Hi-Tech Toilets. 'I must say, my factory looks better without that eyesore.'

'Yes, we'll start clearing the site tomorrow,' said Dave.

Finn was about to launch himself through the mist, fists flying, screaming, 'Murderer!' when suddenly a voice said '*Pssst!*' close to his ear. He spun round. A hand clamped over his mouth before he could cry out, 'Mr Brush! You're alive!'

They both stayed like that, listening to the footsteps of Dave and the MD walking away. They heard cars driving off. It was only then that Mr Brush took his hand away.

'You're alive!' gasped Finn. 'What about Superloo and Blaster?'

'They're both safe.'

'Thank goodness,' said Finn. 'I thought, I thought . . .'

'You thought we were buried under that rubble?' said Mr Brush grimly. 'Well, we would have been if Superloo hadn't saved us. That toilet was a hero last night.'

'What happened?' Finn wanted to ask. But he was still dazed by what he was seeing. His mind just couldn't take it in. Yesterday, there'd been a building here and now it was just a heap of bricks. Here and there in the debris other things poked out – a fragment of pretty blue-flowered porcelain. Mr Brush recognized it all too well. That toilet had been the prize of his collection. The great Thomas Crapper's Deluge, now smashed to pieces.

He picked the fragment up and gently blew off the brick dust. And, for the first time, Finn fully realized what an awful blow this was for Mr Brush. It made his own hair problems fade into insignificance. Mr Brush had lost his home and, more than that, his life's work.

'Your toilet collection?' Finn asked. 'Did you save anything?'

'We didn't have time,' sighed Mr Brush. 'We even lost Superloo's relatives – the ones you brought back from your time-travelling trips.'

Finn had never seen the old man so beaten down, so despondent. He felt really sorry for him. It scared him too. Mr Brush seemed to have lost all his fighting spirit. And if Mr Lew Brush gave up, how could any of them go on?

'We'll search through the rubble!' Finn blurted out desperately. 'We'll find all the pieces. Stick them together!'

Mr Brush shook his head sadly. He let the fragment of toilet fall back on to the rubble pile. 'I just haven't got the heart,' he explained. 'And besides, it won't be the same.'

Finn was desperate to cheer him up. But what could he do? Suddenly, he remembered something. He scrabbled in his pocket. 'I know it's not much,' he said, 'but I brought something back for you from Tudor times.' And he held out that little silver bullet in the palm of his hand.

'An antimony pill!' cried Mr Brush. 'Where'd you get it?'

'From Dr Slide's lodgings,' said Finn. 'He was King Henry's physician.'

'Amazing!' said Mr Brush. His eyes sparkled again as if his passion for toilets and all things toilet-related had suddenly been rekindled.

'Do you know what an antimony pill is?' he asked Finn excitedly.

'*Errr*, no, actually.'

'Well, it's a pill made of metal. And when you swallow it, it cures constipation, makes you rush to the loo.'

'Oh, right,' said Finn. That was already way more information than he needed.

But Lew Brush was rushing on: 'And these pills were precious! I mean, antimony was an expensive metal and, of course, your stomach couldn't digest it, so you collected it when it came out the other end. And reused it!'

'Pardon?' said Finn, not sure if he'd understood.

'Whole families shared one pill. It got passed around then handed down from generation to generation, like a family heirloom!'

'*Yuk!*' said Finn, who'd understood now and wished he hadn't. 'You mean someone swallowed it, then pooed it out, then someone else swallowed it again? That's revolting!'

'I expect they washed it in between,' said Mr Lew Brush.

'It's still revolting!' said Finn, trying not to imagine taking turns with the pill after his big brother. 'You mean whole families used that and I've been carrying it around in my pocket?'

'Probably not whole families with this one,' said Mr Brush. 'This one is really special. From where you found it, I expect it's the personal pill of King Henry himself.'

'*Urrgh!*' said Finn. 'You mean that came out of King Henry's bottom?'

'Probably many, many times,' said Mr Brush. 'It's well known the King was plagued with constipation.'

Finn practically threw the pill at Mr Brush. 'Here, you take it!'

'Thank you, Finn,' said Mr Brush gratefully. 'Thank you for bringing me this treasure. I'm sorry I got so down. It was unforgivable! I realize now I must go on! Never give up, eh, Finn? This pill shall be the start of my new collection!'

Finn felt a warm glow inside because he'd given Mr Brush hope again. He reckoned he could now ask, 'What happened last night?'

Mr Brush began by telling Finn about the message on the Net from the lonely ladies' toilet.

'Superloo didn't answer, did it?' said Finn, who'd been warned countless times about dodgy people on the Net pretending to be who they weren't.

'I'm afraid it did, before I could stop it,' said Mr Brush. 'It wanted to meet a loo like itself *so* much.'

Finn nodded in complete understanding: 'I know.'

'Anyway, it was a trap of, course. They just wanted to track it down. Someone came to get it.'

'Who? Soldiers?'

'No,' said Mr Brush. 'Just one bloke. I was checking around and I saw him through the tool shed window. He'd set up a laptop. He didn't see me, so I crept back into the museum. Superloo was going barmy yelling, "My love has replied! She's waiting out in the tool shed." So I was arguing with it, trying to persuade it there was no lonely ladies' toilet; they just wanted to terminate it. But you know how stubborn it is . . .' Finn nodded again. Mr Brush didn't have to tell him about that.

'Anyway, at that moment there was this terrific crash and the first wrecking ball smashed into the front of the Toilet Museum. And, after that, it was just mayhem!'

Mr Brush couldn't help reliving it all in his mind – the museum disintegrating around him, bricks raining down. There was choking dust. And Superloo screamed, 'Get into my cubicle!' He'd taken cover with Blaster. Then Superloo took off, dodging the flying debris as if it was space junk, and went whirling into the past.

'Where did you go?' asked Finn.

'I don't know. Even Superloo doesn't know – it didn't have time to set time coordinates. We got really shaken up inside. And Blaster got upset, and you know what happens . . .'

Finn nodded, quickly this time. 'I know.' He didn't want any more details about that – he was still feeling queasy about that antimony pill.

'So Superloo managed to stabilize and it hovered in time for a bit and then we came back.'

'Where to?' asked Finn.

'To my allotment. That's where Superloo is now, with Blaster.'

'But what about this guy, the one with the laptop who set the trap? What happened to him?'

'I don't know. The tool shed got flattened too. I was just going to look when the MD turned up.'

Mr Lew Brush frowned uneasily as they picked their way round the big rubble mountain to the small pile of rubble that had once been the tool shed. The bloke they'd sent to terminate Superloo had been very strange. Anonymous really. Mr Brush could hardly remember what he looked like – grey suit, sandy hair, a face with not one distinguishing feature. Except for his eyes. Mr Bush remembered those, as the guy sat in the tool shed, typing out that reply, pretending to be a ladies' toilet. His eyes were chilling. Totally focussed and fanatical.

Mr Lew Brush poked the collapsed tool shed with his foot. He heaved up a corner of the corrugated iron 'He's under here! The roof fell on him!' He heaved the roof up further and toppled it over to reveal Hans Dryer's body. 'Don't look, Finn. His head's a bit of a mess.'

Then Finn heard Mr Lew Brush say, 'Well I never!' So Finn looked, steeling himself for a gory scene. But there was no blood at all or brains. Hans Dryer's skull was smashed open – but it was stuffed with circuitry and microchips. Finn gulped. It was still a very creepy sight.

'It's a robot!' said Mr Brush. 'One of those bionic ones, built to look like a human.'

'Is it still working?' asked Finn, coming forward to kick Mr Hans Dryer's pale, floppy hand with his foot.

'No,' said Mr Lew Brush. 'Its computer brain is wrecked. It's no danger to Superloo any more.'

'What are you going to do?' asked Finn. 'I mean, about the body?'

'Nothing,' said Mr Brush, lowering the iron sheet over the robot assassin. 'It's just a machine after all. And someone must have sent it – let them sort it out. Come on, I'll take you to my allotment. It's just down the road.'

On the way, Finn asked how Superloo was. Like Mr Brush, the great toilet genius had had a bad time. It must be devastated. It had been disappointed in love and it had lost all its toilet relatives.

'Well, all right, considering,' was Mr Brush's surprising answer. 'I thought up another little scheme to make it mobile. A better one this time.' They walked through the big iron gates that led into the allotments. Mr Brush said, 'Mine's over there. I've got a little shed. It's quite cosy.'

Finn peered through the fog – he could hardly see a thing. Then '*Aaaargh!*' he cried, leaping back.

Out of the mist floated a great silver ghost, hovering above the sprouts and cabbages. It drifted off into the fog, then appeared spookily again among the pea sticks. 'Don't be scared!' quacked a familiar voice. 'It's ME. Superloo. I'm a *hoverloo* now!'

Later, back at the Hi-Tech Toilets factory, when the fog had cleared, a helicopter appeared. There was a whirlwind, a loud *JUD JUD JUD*, and it landed next to the ruins of the Toilet Museum. Men in combat gear came sprinting out with a stretcher. They lifted the mangled remains of Mr Hans Dryer on to it, not forgetting his laptop, and raced back with him to the 'copter. The robot, who'd been specially built to hunt other robots and programmed to hate them but had no idea he was a robot himself, was whirled away into the blue. It was a very slick operation, all over in minutes.

Was he repairable? Could he resume the hunt for Superloo? Only the robotic experts who made him could tell.

Finn said, '*Wow!* That hovering thing you do is terrific!'

He was proud of Superloo. It was irrepressible! It could have plunged into gloom after its recent disappointments but, like Mr Brush, it had bounced back. It was thrilled with the hover cushion that inflated on its bottom, allowing it to float around. Its sensors made sure it avoided obstacles and didn't bump into anything.

'I'm flying!' it cried as it hovered into Mr Brush's shed, where he was brewing Finn and himself some tea. A sudden rude, trumping sound filled the shed, as if someone had sat on a whoopee cushion.

'Was that you, Blaster?' asked Mr Brush.

'It was ME!' cried Superloo. It did it again, more loudly this time. *TERRR-RUMP!*

'It's that hover cushion deflating,' said Mr Brush. 'I'll have to do something about that.' But Superloo wasn't at all embarrassed. It was delighted with its new mobility.

'The next time-travelling trip we go on,' it told Finn excitedly, 'I shall be able to come with you everywhere! I could come with you NOW, to the park, to the pictures!'

'*Errr*, I don't think that's a good idea,' said Finn tactfully. Other kids went out with their mates. Going out with a public convenience? How sad was that?

'Anyway,' Finn said, 'we've only just come

back from Tudor times.' He still hadn't shaken off the experience. He'd never forget meeting King Henry or the sinister Dr Slide. But most of all, he'd remember Tib and Toby. 'What happened to them and Sir Percival?' he wondered.

But Superloo was pondering something else. 'Honestly, I could kick myself,' it quacked.

'What's the matter now?' said Finn.

'Well, I never asked, did I?' said Superloo. 'I never asked the Groom of the Stool, *Did you, or did you not, wipe the King's bum?*'

Mr Lew Brush shook his head solemnly. 'That question,' he said, 'will forever remain one of the great unsolved mysteries of toilet history.'

## What happened back in Tudor times?

Roger reappeared up a palace privy!

Sir Percival left Court. It was far too dangerous!
Tib and Toby became his wards and lived with
him on his country estate.

Dr Slide never returned to Court either.
He made a living peddling quack medicines
at country fairs.

# OFF WITH THEIR HEADS!

Two of Henry VIII's wives had their heads cut off. But which ones?

# SPOT THE DIFFERENCE
## Twelve things are different in these drawings – but what are they?

*Answers are at the bottom of the page.*

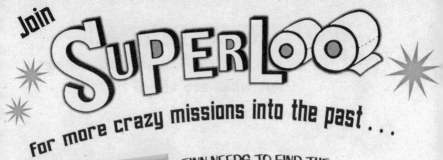

Join **SUPERLOO**

*for more crazy missions into the past . . .*

FINN NEEDS TO FIND THE LEGENDARY GOLDEN TOILET OF KING TUTANKHAMUN – CAN HE PASS HIMSELF OFF AS AN ANCIENT EGYPTIAN TO GET IT BACK?

SUPERLOO HAS TAKEN FINN TO ROMAN BRITAIN WHERE CONSPIRACIES ARE AFOOT INVOLVING GLADIATORS, BEARS, VERY FIERCE BRITISH TRIBES AND, OF COURSE . . . HADRIAN'S FAMOUS LATRINE.

Can Superloo escape capture and termination?

What will its next mission be?

Will Finn change his mind and go with it?

puffin.co.uk